FADING INTO SILENCE

NICHOLAS MICHAEL MATIZ

Copyright © 2024 by Nicholas Michael Matiz

All rights reserved.

No part of this book may be reproduced in any form or by any electronic or mechanical means, including information storage and retrieval systems, without written permission from the author, except for the use of brief quotations in a book review.

For my family

CONTENTS

Introduction — vii

1. Right Onto Me — 1
2. The Night We Danced — 7
3. Sex, Whiskey, & Family — 13
4. The Task — 17
5. Scandalous — 25
6. Never Enough To Daddy — 28
7. For Mother — 31
8. Roulette — 35
9. An Idea — 39
10. The Break-Up — 42
11. Secrets Revealed — 48
12. Wine, Wine, Wine — 55
13. Loose Ends — 60
14. Confessions — 66
15. Feels Like This — 69
16. Roll With It — 74
17. Recycling — 82
18. Home — 85
19. The Letter — 88
20. Freedom — 91

Afterword — 95
Stay Tuned — 97
About the Author — 99

INTRODUCTION

Fading Into Silence isn't just a tale of love and crime; it's a raw exploration of family loyalty, power, and identity in a world that constantly demands more than it gives. At its core, this story delves into the complex bonds that hold people together, even as those same bonds slowly destroy them.

Set against the backdrop of 1980s Los Angeles, where the lines between ambition and corruption blur, we meet Jace and Clay—two men who are both products of their environments and rebel against it. Jace, trapped in the violent grasp of his criminal family, struggles to reconcile his love for Clay with the loyalty that ties him to his brother, Cole. Clay, searching for freedom and meaning outside his wealthy yet distant family, is drawn into a world of danger and deceit he never anticipated. Together, they navigate a world where survival often means sacrifice, and love can become a double-edged sword.

The extremes in *Fading Into Silence*—from intense family drama to brutal violence—are not simply fictional exaggerations but necessary elements that highlight the emotional and psychological weight of the characters' decisions. This story captures the intensity of what it means to choose between love and loyalty, self-preservation and self-destruction, especially when the stakes are life or death. These extremes serve to reflect the heightened realities of human experience, pushing the characters—and the readers—into uncomfortable but necessary territory.

Through the chaos of Jace and Clay's journey, Fading Into Silence asks an important question: How far would you go to protect the ones you love, and at what point does loyalty become a prison?

In this gritty, unapologetic debut narrative from Nicholas Michael Matiz, family loyalty isn't just tested—it's shattered, leaving the characters, and us, to pick up the pieces and question what it means to belong in a world that can—and will—go on without you.

1

RIGHT ONTO ME

CLAY

1986 — California

THE MIRROR in my bathroom has seen more of me than most lovers ever will. Every crack in its surface tells a story, a sliver of time where I stood, naked in the half-light, examining the person I've become. I trace my fingers over the edge of the glass, cool and sharp, just enough to feel alive. That's the thing about this life--every moment cuts, just deep enough to remind me that the scars aren't fading.

Every heartbeat pulses with the weight of mistakes, things I should've done differently, words I should've never said. But here I am, standing in front of a broken reflection, half-dressed in the city that never lets me sleep.

You see, the world doesn't care if you're cracked or shattered. Neon lights flash outside my window, a constant reminder that life goes on whether you're ready or not. And me? I'm never fucking ready. But the night drags me in, like an ex who knows your weak spots and knows exactly how to pull you back into the chaos.

I've always been a little too comfortable with chaos. Maybe it's in my blood. My father was the kind of man who would rather punch a wall (or me, depending on his mood) than talk about feelings, and my mother... well, she was long gone before she left.

Tonight, though, it's just me and this reflection. A cigarette dangles between my lips, half-burnt, barely hanging on like the pieces of my sanity.

I take a drag, the smoke filling my lungs, thick and sweet, almost like a lover's kiss. That kiss you know is poison but tastes too damn good to stop. It's the kind of thing you learn to crave when you've been burned by something hotter than fire. When pain starts to feel more like comfort, peace is just another four-letter word you don't trust.

I wasn't always this wrecked. There was a time when I had plans--dreams, even. But life, like an unfaithful partner, has a way of breaking promises. Now, it's just survival. Get through the day. Drown out the voices at night. Wake up and do it all over again.

I stubbed out the cigarette, my fingers lingering on the filter as if holding onto the last piece of something familiar. The mirror still stared back at me, mocking me, reminding me of everything I let slip through my fingers. I was good at that—letting things go. People, places, and pieces of myself that I thought I didn't need anymore. It was easier than holding on, easier than facing what it meant to care.

Call My Name by Michael Bolton is playing on the record player from the living room. I had stumbled upon his 1985 album *Everybody's Crazy* earlier that day in the shop down the street. It reminded me of Jace. This song was the first song we danced to the night we met.

Then there was Jace. As always, sneaking back into my heart.

A shadow of a memory now, but one that still stuck around like the smell of his cologne on my skin. We weren't good for each other—never were. But we were something. Two broken people trying to make sense of each other, when we couldn't even make sense of ourselves. The last time I saw him was three months ago. He told me to get out of his life, and I told myself I didn't care. But that was a lie. I cared then, and I cared now, even if I hated myself for it.

The knock came, sharp and fast, rattling the front door like a warning shot. I froze. Nobody came to my place unannounced, not unless they had a reason. And reasons, I'd learned, usually weren't good.

I left the bathroom and made my way through the hallway and into the living room where the front door was. I hesitated for a second but answered the door.

There he was. *Jace.*

His face was pale, eyes wide with terror, and in his hand —God, no—was a gun. He didn't wait for me to speak and didn't even give me the chance to process what was happening. He shoved past me, slamming the door behind him, chest heaving like he'd been running for hours. The gun waved in his hand, trembling with the same desperation that filled his voice.

"Clay, you gotta help me. You have to, man. He's coming. My brother, he's gonna fucking kill me!"

I stared at him, mouth open, but no words came out. Jace, standing in my apartment, looking like a man about to lose everything. I didn't know whether to scream at him for showing up or pull him into my arms and tell him everything would be okay. But nothing was okay, and deep down I knew it.

"Jace, what the hell are you talking about?" I managed, my voice breaking in a way that betrayed me. I wanted to be angry, but all I felt was that damn pull—that love I never shook off, not after all this time.

"I fucked up, Clay. My brother—he found out. About us. About everything." His voice cracked. "He's coming to kill me. I swear to God."

Before I could say anything, before I could even think, the door burst open. Splintered wood flew across the room, and then I saw him. Jace's brother. Eyes wild, shotgun raised. There was no time. The blast came with a deafening roar, and fire exploded in my shoulder.

I spun around, crashing into the glass coffee table behind me, shards tearing into my skin as I hit the floor. The pain was instant and blinding, my breath caught somewhere between a scream and a gasp. I tried to focus, to move, but my body wouldn't listen.

I lay there, bleeding out on the floor, gasping for air that wouldn't come. My vision blurred, and the room spun, the once-familiar apartment now a nightmare I couldn't wake up from. The sharp smell of blood mixed with smoke and broken glass, thick in the air, as my chest tightened with panic. I wanted to scream Jace's name, tell him to run, to get out before it was too late.

But my voice was lost in the chaos.

Michael Bolton continued to sing.

Jace.

He was standing there, frozen in the middle of the room, staring at his brother like a deer caught in headlights. His cheatheaved with quick, terrified breaths. I could see it in his eyes—the mix of fear and disbelief, as if he couldn't comprehend what was happening. As if his brother wasn't standing there, gun smoking, hatred boiling over in his eyes.

"Faggot," his brother snarled, the word dripping with venom. And then the second blast.

I watched it happen in slow motion. The way Jace's body jolted backward, chest blown open as if it had been ripped apart by a force too cruel to exist. His mouth opened in a silent scream, eyes wide with shock and pain. He stumbled, arms reaching out as if trying to grab onto something, anything to stop the inevitable. And then he fell.

Right onto me.

The weight of him crushed against my chest, his blood spilling onto my shirt, mixing with mine. My hands instinctively went to him, trying to hold him, keep him there with me, but he was limp, lifeless. The gun fell from his hand, clattering to the floor beside us, the sound barely registering through the ringing in my ears.

"Jace," I whispered, or at least I thought I did. My voice was weak, barely audible over the pounding in my skull. I tried to move, tried to push myself up, but the pain in my shoulder shot through me like a thousand knives, pinning me to the ground.

His brother was still there, standing over us, breathing heavily, his face twisted with rage and something else—satisfaction. The shotgun hung loosely in his hands, like a tool that had done its job. His eyes flickered down to me for a moment, as if debating whether to finish the job or just let me bleed out with Jace.

But he didn't say a word. He turned, storming out of the apartment, leaving the door wide open behind him, as if this scene—the blood, the bodies, the shattered glass—meant nothing. Like we meant nothing.

I lay there, now beginning to choke on my blood, staring up at the cracked ceiling. Jace's body was heavy on mine, his face inches from mine. I could smell the familiar scent of his skin, his hair, the faint trace of cigarettes and cologne that used to cling to him like a second skin.

And all I could think about, as the darkness crept closer, was how much I loved him.

I always loved him. Even when I hated him. Even when he left. Even now, with him dying on top of me, his blood mixing with mine, his body ever so limp. I loved him, and that was the one thing I couldn't escape.

The world started to fade, the edges of my vision going dark, my heartbeat slowing in my chest. And in that moment, as the pain dulled and the coldness set in, I didn't care about anything else. Not the anger, not the mistakes, not the years we lost.

All that mattered was that I loved him. And in some fucked up way, at least he was here, with me. At least we weren't alone.

The last thing I felt before everything went black was Jace's weight on my chest, his heartbeat fading into silence.

2

THE NIGHT WE DANCED

CLAY

1985 - California

I SAT IN MY APARTMENT, staring at the ceiling, feeling emptier than usual. A year before everything went to hell, and I was already drowning in loneliness. It wasn't the kind you could fix with company or distraction—no, this was a deeper kind of loneliness that settled in your bones and wouldn't leave.

I needed to get out, needed to feel alive. The streets of Downtown LA were too quiet for what I had in mind. West Hollywood—it was loud, dirty, and crowded with people who didn't give a damn. Perfect. I grabbed my leather jacket, slipped it over my shoulders, and slung my leg over my bike. The engine roared to life beneath me, vibrating against my thighs as I sped down the highway, weaving through traffic like it didn't matter if I made it home or not.

357—a gay bar—was my usual spot. Some dive bar with sticky floors, dim lights, and bartenders who didn't ask questions. Exactly what I needed tonight. When I walked in, the scent of stale beer and cigarettes hit me, and I felt that familiar buzz start in my chest. It wasn't happiness, not even close, but it was something. I slid onto a stool, signaling the bartender with a nod.

"Whiskey. Keep 'em coming," I said, my voice rougher than I'd meant it to be.

I threw back the first shot, wincing as the burn spread down my throat, warming my chest. It wasn't enough. It never was, but it dulled the edges of loneliness and made it easier to forget. I kept drinking, my head getting lighter with each round, my grip on the world loosening.

That's when he walked in.

Jace. I didn't know him yet, of course, but he had that look—messy hair, eyes that looked like they'd seen too much, and a confidence that came with being pissed off at the world. He walked like he didn't give a damn, like nothing could touch him, and I was drawn to it, like a moth to a flame. He sat down right next to me, even though the bar was half empty.

"Whiskey," he said to the bartender, glancing at me sideways with a smirk. "I take it we're on the same page tonight. I'm Jace."

I laughed, more out of surprise than anything else. "Yeah, something like that. Just trying to forget the world for a while. Clay, here."

"Aren't we all?" he said, clinking his glass against mine. "Here's to bad decisions."

It wasn't long before the conversation flowed as easily as

the whiskey. We talked about nothing and everything all at once. He told me about the shitty apartment he lived in, the kind with walls so thin you could hear your neighbors breathing, and I told him about my bike, how I rode it just to feel something, anything, other than the numbness that followed me around like a shadow.

"You know," he said after a while, leaning closer, his breath warm against my ear, "you don't seem like the type to let life get you down. You've got that 'badass' thing going."

I chuckled, feeling the heat rise in my chest, maybe from the whiskey or maybe from him. "Yeah? And you've got that 'mysterious stranger who's about to ruin my life' thing going on. I like it."

He laughed, low and rough, and something inside me shifted. That loneliness I'd been growing in—it didn't feel so heavy anymore. I hadn't come here looking for anything, but somehow, I found him.

A few songs played on the jukebox, but it wasn't until *Call My Name* by Michael Bolton started to play that the night changed. He looked at me, eyes soft in a way I hadn't seen before. "You know, it'd be a crime not to dance to this."

I blinked, not expecting the offer, but the alcohol had me feeling bold. "You serious?"

"Hell yeah," he grinned, standing up and offering me his hand. "Come on. It's not like anyone's watching."

We stumbled to the dance floor, both of us drunk, both laughing like idiots, but it didn't matter. He pulled me close, our bodies swaying awkwardly to the ballad, and for the first time in years, I felt...happy. Stupidly, inexplicably happy.

"Not bad for a couple of drunks," I teased, my forehead pressing against his.

"Yeah, well, you've got moves I wasn't expecting," he shot back, that cocky grin never leaving his face.

When the song ended, we didn't pull away. He looked at me like he was seeing me for the first time, and I felt it too. Something deep, something I hadn't felt before. Or maybe I'd felt it once and forgot what it was like, Either way, I wasn't letting go.

"You wanna get out of here?" he asked.

"Yeah. Let's go."

We hopped on my bike, the city blurring past us as I drove us back to my place. Neither of us said a word the whole ride, the tension between us heavy in the air. By the time, we stumbled through my front door, the world outside didn't exist anymore.

We barely made it through the door before our lips crashed together. It wasn't gentle, wasn't soft—it was urgent, messy, like two people who had been holding back for too long. His hands gripped the back of my neck, pulling me closer, while mine found the hem of his shirt, tugging it off without a second thought.

I kicked the door shut behind us, pressing him against the wall, my breath ragged, my heart pounding in my chest. He tasted like whiskey, like every bad decision I'd ever made wrapped into one perfect moment. His fingers slid under my jacket, yanking it off my shoulders, and for the first time in my life, the world outside didn't matter. There was no loneliness, no emptiness—just him and me, and the heat building between us.

"You sure about this?" he whispered, his voice ever so low, rough, like he was barely holding on.

I answered him the only way I knew how—by kissing him harder, deeper, letting him know I was more than sure. This wasn't just about the drinks or the thrill of the night. It was about something neither of us could put into words yet, something that had been simmering the moment we sat next to each other at the bar.

We stumbled our way to the bed, half-laughing, half-breathless, peeling off the rest of our clothes like we couldn't get close enough. His hands roamed over my skin, sending shivers down my spine as he pushed me down onto the mattress. For a moment, his gaze locked on mine, something more than lust in his eyes—something deeper, more dangerous.

"God, you're beautiful," he said, his voice soft I almost didn't hear it.

I laughed, breathless. "You don't have to butter me up. You already got me here."

His lips curved into a grin, but there was something real behind it, something that made my chest tighten. He leaned down, pressing a slow, lingering kiss against my lips, and suddenly it wasn't just about the hunger anymore. It was about connection. About being seen.

Our bodies over together, the heat between us growing with every touch, every gasp, every whispered name. It was like nothing I'd ever felt before—intense and tender all at once like we'd been waiting our whole lives for this moment. He wasn't just anyone, and I wasn't just looking for a way to fill the void anymore.

Time blurred, our breaths coming in sync, the room spinning in that way it does when everything feels so good to be real. And when it was over, when finally collapsed next to each other, neither of us said a word. There was no need.

He turns to me, his arm draped lazily over my chest, his fingers tracing patterns on my skin. I lit a cigarette and we shared it. I stared up at the ceiling, feeling more alive than I had in years like maybe I wasn't so lost after all. Like maybe I'd finally found something worth holding onto.

"So, is this the part where we pretend this never happened?" I asked, trying to keep it light, though the question weighed heavier than I intended.

Jace chuckled, shaking his head. "No chance. You're not getting rid of me that easily."

I smiled at that, a real smile, the kind I hadn't felt in longer than I cared to admit. We lay there in silence, the world outside my apartment fading into nothing as if this moment—this night—was the only thing that existed.

I didn't know what tomorrow would bring, or if this was just a fleeting moment of connection before we went back to our separate lives. But for now, lying there next to him, with the warmth of his body against mine, I didn't care.

For the first time, I wasn't lonely.

For the first time, I didn't want to be anywhere else.

3

SEX, WHISKEY, & FAMILY

JACE

Next Day

The morning sun filtered through the thin curtains, casting soft shadows across Clay's bare chest. I lay beside him, the sheets tangled around our legs and watched as his chest rose and fell with each breath. It was quiet, that perfect kind ofsilence where the world outside doesn't exist—just two people, still tangled in the night before. My arm draped over his stomach, fingers absentmindedly tracing circles in his skin. I knew we had to talk eventually, but for now, I just wanted to stay in this moment.

"That was one hell of a night," Clay mumbled, his voice thick with sleep, a lazy grin stretching across his face as he opened his eyes to meet mine.

"Yeah, well, Michael Bolton does things to people," I said with a smirk. "He's like some kind of love wizard."

Clay chuckled softly, rolling onto his side to face me. "I'm starting to think you're the one who put a spell on me."

I raised an eyebrow, leaning in to press a kiss to his lips, slow and teasing. "Maybe I did."

We lay there for a while, wrapped in each other, until reality started creeping in. I could feel it—the weight of everything I hadn't told him yet. My family, the things I was caught up in, the reason I usually kept people at arm's length. But something about Clay made me want to let him in, even if just a little.

"My family," I started, my voice quieter than before, "they're...not exactly the kind of people you'd bring home to meet your mom. Not that I'm planning on scaring you off or anything, but they've got their hands in some...shady shit. Drugs, mostly."

Clay didn't flinch, just watched me with those soft, curious eyes. "You're not scaring me away," he said after a moment, his hand sliding up my arm. "But I get it. Family's complicated."

I nodded, feeling the tension in my chest loosens slightly. "Yeah. Complicated is a good word for it. I've spent most of my life trying to stay out of their mess, but it's not exactly easy when they've got a grip on the whole city."

Clay shifted closer to me, his leg brushing against mine. "I don't have that problem. My family's got money, but they cut me off a long time ago. I get a check every month, enough to live on, but that's it. No phone calls, no holidays, just cash." He laughed, though it didn't reach his eyes. "Guess we both got dealt some shitty hands, huh?"

I smiled, leaning over to kiss him again, my lips lingering on his for a moment longer than before. "We make a good pair, don't we? The black sheep of our respective fucked-up families."

"Guess so," he murmured against my lips, his hands already pulling me closer. We didn't need to say anything more after that. The conversation melted away as we got lost in each other again, the same heat from the night before surging back, stronger now, even more urgent. We made love, slow and deep like we were trying to carve out a space for ourselves in a world that didn't care if we existed.

Afterward, we drank more whiskey, a new bottle half-empty by the time we stumbled back out to the living room. Clay turned on the radio he kept on the side table by the couch and *Desperate Heart* started playing, Michael Bolton's voice filling the room like it was made just for us. We smiled at the odds of Bolton playing again. We danced, the same drunken sways and stumbles, laughing as we whispered pieces of the lyrics to each other.

"You're the only one who could break my heart," Clay slurred, his arms wrapped around my neck, eyes bright with that drunken sparkle. "That's so us, isn't it?"

"Yeah," I agreed, pulling him closer, my lips brushing his ear. "But don't go breaking mine, alright?"

The next day, we decided to escape the city and head out to Malibu. The drive was easy, Clay's bike slithering around cars, the ocean breeze cutting through the hangover that clung to us both. When we hit the beach, we found a quiet spot and stretched out on the sand, the waves crashing nearby as we let the sun warm our skin.

"I've been thinking," I said after a while, breaking the comfortable silence. "There's a way…a way we could make something of ourselves. Not just get by on whiskey and beach days."

Clay turned his head to look at me, eyebrows raised in curiosity. "What do you mean?"

I hesitated for a second, but I could see it in his eyes—he was all in, whatever I had to say. "My brother. He's deep in the family business and knows how to move money, product, whatever. If we talk to him and get in good…we could be set. No more checks from your family, no more scraping by."

To my surprise, Clay didn't hesitate. He nodded, a grin spreading across his face. "I'm in. I don't want to just sit on the sidelines anymore. I want to be a part of something bigger. With you."

I smiled, feeling something stir in my chest. "Alright then. I'll set up a meeting."

4

THE TASK

C LAY

A Week Later

A week passed, and the memory of that Malibu day still clung to me like saltwater on my skin. I'd been restless ever since, replaying Jace's words about his brother and the "business" over and over in my mind. It wasn't just the idea of joining something bigger that had me on edge—it was the thought of me being tied to him, to Jace, in a way that went deeper than whiskey-fueled nights and Michael Bolton songs.

I was half-expecting him to disappear on me after that conversation. Maybe it was all just talk, a wild idea born from too much sun and booze. But then, I got the call.

"Meet me in Palm Springs. Here's the address," Jace had

said, his voice steady, like we were about to grab a drink and not potentially change the course of our lives. There was something about the calmness in his tone that made my stomach twist.

Now here I was, standing outside a mansion that looked straight out of a Hollywood set. Palms lined the driveway, and the desert heat beat down on my leather jacket. I should've ditched it, but nerves had me sticking to what felt familiar. This place was unreal—huge white walls, perfectly manicured lawns, and a sleek black car parked out front that probably cost more than my entire life.

Jace stood by the front door, leaning casually against the frame with that same easy grin I'd come to love and hate at the same time. He waved me over, and as I got closer, I could see a spark of excitement in his eyes.

"About time you showed up," he teased, pulling me in for a quick kiss, looking behind him briefly. I noted it but didn't make much of it. "Ready to meet the family?"

"I'm ready for a drink," I joked, though my heart was racing.

He laughed, taking my hand and leading me inside. The mansion was even more ridiculous on the inside—marble floors, high ceilings, and art that looked like it belonged in a museum. We passed through a spacious living room where a man was lounging on an expensive-looking sofa, sipping something—wine?— out of a crystal glass.

"That's him," Jace whispered, nodding toward the man. "My brother, Cole."

Cole looked exactly like the kind of guy you'd expect to be running things behind the scenes in LA—slick, confident, with that dangerous charm you couldn't quite trust. He had Jace's sharp jawline and dark hair, but his eyes were colder, calculating.

"Clay right?" Cole said, standing up and extending a hand. His grip was firm, and I could feel the weight of his gaze as he sized me up. I thought he lingered on my crotch for a moment longer than he should've but he could've been scanning for a weapon. "Jace's told me a lot about you."

"All good things, I hope," I replied, forcing a smile.

Cole chuckled. He glanced at Jace. "Mostly."

Before I could even think of a comeback, another man entered the room. He was older, dressed in a suit that screamed money, and had this easy charisma that made you instantly want to like him. I recognized him immediately—Steven Barnes, a big-name Hollywood producer. I'd seen his name in credits more times than I could count.

"And this is Steven," Jace said, introducing the producer like he was just some regular guy at a backyard a backyard barbecue. "He's a close...business partner of ours."

Steven gave me a charming smile, his handshake softer than Cole's but no less calculated. "Pleasure to meet you, Clay. I've heard great things."

I nodded, trying to play it cool but it was hard not to feel like I was in over my head. We all moved outside to the backyard, where a private chef was preparing a three-course meal on a long wooden table overlooking the desert landscape. The whole thing felt surreal—like I'd stepped into someone else's life, someone who was used to wealth and power in ways I'd only ever seen from a distance. Despite my own wealthy family.

As we sat down, Cole wasted no time diving into the conversation, laying out how things worked, and how their "business" ran through the film industry and across the city. Steven chimed in, explaining how Hollywood was the perfect cover for moving product—so much money, so many people, no one ever questioned a thing.

Jace sat next to me, his hand casually—hidden?—resting on my thigh under the table, a subtle reassurance that I wasn't in this alone. "We've been thinking," Cole said, cutting into his steak with precise motion, "about how you could fit into all this. Jace seems to think you've got potential."

I swallowed, trying not to let my nerves show. "I'm not afraid of getting my hands dirty if that's what you're asking."

Cole smirked. "Good. Because we've got a little job for you two. Think of it as a test."

Jace's grip on my thigh tightened slightly, and I knew whatever was coming next was big.

"We need you to plant some evidence," Cole continued, his voice now low and firm. "In the current mayor's office. He's becoming a problem. My uncle's running against him, and we can't afford any competition."

My heart pounded in my chest as I processed his words. Planting evidence? In the mayor's office? This was beyond anything I'd imagined when Jace brought up his family. But as crazy as it sounded, there was something about it that excited me—like I was finally part of something, finally on the inside.

Jace looked at me. Eyes searching for a sign. Of what exactly, I don't know. Perhaps I'll never know. "You in?"

I glanced at him, then at Cole and Steven. The air was thick with anticipation, waiting for my answer. "Yeah," I said, my voice steady. "I'm in."

Cole smiled, a dangerous glint in his eyes. "Good. Then let's get to work."

The engine of my bike rumbled beneath me as I roared down the highway, the desert heat still clinging to my skin. The sun had just started to dip below the horizon, casting a golden glow over the empty road ahead of me. Couldn't help but smile, feeling more alive than I had in years. Palm Springs was already behind me, but the excitement of what lay ahead made the ride feel like a victory lap.

Jace and I were in this together now—no more drifting, no more uncertainty. We had a job, a purpose, something bigger than the endless nights of whiskey and dancing. I pictured him beside me, the way his lips felt when we kissed, the way we'd laughed at the bar, our bodies pressed together as we stumbled through that Bolton song. It was all perfect, and I felt like I was finally part of something real.

I gunned the throttle, the wind whipping against my face, the roar of the engine drowning out everything else.

JACE

I sat on the edge of the bed, my hands trembling as I undid the buttons of my shirt. The room was dimly lit, casting shadows across the lavish furniture. I could hear Steven behind me, snorting lines of coke off the glass bedside table. My stomach ached, a bit forming deep inside me, but I kept my expression neutral. This was part of the deal. This is what Cole had set up. The task.

"Relax, Jace," Steven's voice was smooth, like it belonged to someone in control of everything. "We're all just having a little fun here."

I nodded, though my throat felt tight. I could feel the weight of Steven's gaze on my bare skin as I shrugged off my shirt and dropped it to the floor. The air felt thick, and suffocating, and I couldn't bring myself to look at him. Instead, I stared at the bedspread, the rich fabric feeling foreign under my hands. The soft click of a lighter and the smell of cigarette smoke filled the air as Steven took a drag.

CLAY

I LEANED INTO THE BIKE, the wind biting my face, but it didn't matter. Nothing could pull me out of this high. This—this feeling of speed and freedom—was everything. I couldn't stop thinking about Jace, about how much we'd been through in such a short time. The late-night conversations, the shared whiskey, the way we looked at me like I was more than just some rich kid with a broken past.

In my mind, I could see us lying together, tangled in the sheets, the weight of his body pressed against mine. The way he'd kiss me, slow and sweet, like we had all the time in the world.

JACE

THE BED SHIFTED beneath me as Steven climbed on, his hands rough and impatient as they pulled me closer. I swallowed hard, trying to block out the sound of his breathing, the way his fingers dug into my skin. I squeezed my eyes shut, tears already threatening to spill, but I couldn't let them. Not here. Not now.

Behind Steven, in the mirror above the dresser in front of me, I could see Cole sitting in the corner of the room, a glass of wine in his hand, watching. His eyes never left me, cold and detached, like I was just another piece of business. I wanted to scream at him, to beg him to make it stop, but I knew better. This was part of the price.

The mattress creaked as Steven pushed me further into it, his breath hot on the back of my neck. My face jolted forward, and the tears finally slipped free, falling silently onto the bedspread.

CLAY

I SMILED as I pictured us at that bar, Jace laughing as we danced, stumbling over each other's feet, both too drunk to care. His smile was the kind of thing that lit up a room—something I couldn't get enough of. The way he looked at me like I was all he wanted, made me feel invincible.

The city skyline was closer now, the lights growing brighter as I sped toward it. I had no idea what lay ahead for us, what this job would turn into, but no none of that mattered. Not really. As long as we had each other, I knew we'd make it work. Whatever it took.

JACE

I BIT DOWN on my lip, drawing blood, trying to block the pain, the humiliation, the weight of Steven on top of me. I kept my eyes locked on Cole, his silhouette in the corner, sipping his wine like this was some kind of twisted performance.

My mind flashed to Clay, to the way he'd held me in bed just a week ago. He had no idea what was happening right now, what I was doing for us, for him. I couldn't let him know. I couldn't let this touch him.

Another jolt and my head snapped forward again, my vision blurring with more tears.

5

SCANDALOUS

JACE

Two Weeks Later

We were at Mel's Diner on Sunset, the neon sign flickering as we slid into a red booth by the window. It was late, the kind of LA night where the city felt endless, buzzing with the energy of people who couldn't sleep or didn't want to. Clay sat across from me, his fingers drumming on the edge of his coffee cup, eyes sharp and waiting. He always had that look—ready for whatever came next. And tonight, I had something for him.

"You're gonna like this one," I said, leaning in. I glanced around the diner, making sure no one was listening, but it was just us and a couple of insomniacs nursing pancakes. "The mayor's got a little hobby. He's into hookers."

Clay raised an eyebrow, a slow smile tugging at the corner of his lips. "A politician with a hooker problem? Color me shocked."

I smirked, feeling that familiar thrill I always got when a plan was about to come together. "He's been discreet about it, kinda, but I've got a source. We follow him, catch him in the act, and snap some photos. After that, we'll leave the evidence on his desk—anonymously, of course. With a little note saying 'scandalous.' And a knife for dramatic effect."

Clay's smile widened, his fingers finally stilling. "A knife, huh?"

"Gotta keep it interesting," I said with a shrug. "There's a security guard on our payroll who'll help us get in. The rest is up to us."

Two nights later, we were parked outside some cheap motel on the edge of the city. The kind of place where people went to forget themselves, to pretend they were someone else for a few hours. Sure enough, the mayor showed up around midnight, wearing a hat and sunglasses like he thought he was invisible. We followed him inside, keeping our distance, and watched as he met with a woman who wasn't interested in small talk.

I snapped the photos, careful to stay out of sight, and within an hour, the mayor's little secret was documented and ready to ruin him. We snuck into his office the following night, left the photos and the knife right on his desk, and slipped out like we'd never been there.

The headlines hit the following day: *Mayor Resigns Unexpectedly Amid Scandal*. Turns out, his hooker habit had an even longer history than we thought, and he knew fighting it in court would destroy any chance of keeping his dignity intact. Just like that, the path was cleared for my uncle.

A month later, Cole brought Clay into the fold officially.

He handed us the keys to a gay club in West Hollywood—a little spot called Velvet, nestled between an art gallery and a dive bar. Business was booming, and for a while, it felt like we were untouchable. Nights blurred into mornings, the club packed with bodies, music pounding, drinks flowing. It was everything I'd promised Clay—our slice of the city.

6

NEVER ENOUGH TO DADDY

OLE

A Random Night

The mansion was quiet, a silence that settled into the cracks of the wooden floors and high ceilings. Cole sat in his father's study, staring at the rows of untouched books lining the walls. It was a room designed to project power and intellect, but to him, it just felt like a shrine to everything he'd never be. His father's voice echoed in his head, that constant litany of disappointment and unmet expectations.

"You need to do more, Cole. Be more. This family didn't get here by coasting on your brother's reckless whims. It's time for you to step up."

He poured himself another glass of bourbon, the expensive kind his father always kept in stock, and downed it in one go. It burned going down, but the numbness that followed was familiar, welcome even. No amount of money, drugs, or power ever seemed to dull the sharp edge of his father's words. No matter how many deals he closed or how many people he controlled, it was never enough. He was never enough.

Cole leaned back in the chair, letting the alcohol settle in his bloodstream as he stared up at the ceiling. He should be relieved that Jace and Clay were handling the mayor tonight and that things were moving forward as planned. But the gnawing feeling inside him—the one that had been there since he was a teenager—only grew stronger. It was the same thing that drove him to keep Jace under his thumb, to make his brother suffer in ways that Cole couldn't admit even to himself.

Jace was free in a way Cole could never be. Even if Jace didn't realize it, he had something Cole envied more than anything: the ability to be openly himself. It made Cole sick, the way Jace flaunted his life, his sexuality, without any of the consequences that Cole had lived under every single day. Sure, it wasn't like Jace had it easy—he made sure of that—but at least Jace could have lovers, and could kiss a man in public without caring about what their father thought. Their father never paid attention to Jace. It was like he thought Jace would never be into such heinous acts. Sins.

Cole couldn't. Not with their father always watching, always judging. Not with the weight of the family's expectations pressing down on him, suffocating him. Being gay wasn't just a secret—it was a curse. And no matter how many times he indulged his desires in secret, it was never enough. He would would never be enough. That truth haunted him more than any business deal or family obligation ever could.

The worst part was, that Jace didn't even know how much Cole wanted what he had. He didn't know that every time Cole forced him into degrading situations—like the night with Steven—it was because Cole wanted him to feel the same pain, the same powerlessness that he felt every single day. It wasn't just about control. It was about showing Jace that freedom came with a price.

The 80s had brought with them a wave of AIDS panic, of whispered warnings and fears spreading through the gay community. But Cole barely cared. It wasn't that he didn't understand the danger—it was that it didn't matter. The risk was almost relief, an excuse to push everything further, to test the limits of what little control he had left over his own life.

He drained the last of his bourbon and reached for the bottle again, his hands trembling slightly. He hadn't been okay for years. The drugs, the sex, the money—none of it filled the void. None of it ever made him feel whole. But this —this sick power of Jace—was the only thing that came close to making him feel alive.

Cole wiped his mouth with the back of his hand, the taste of alcohol lingering on his lips as he thought about the random task Jace and Clay were handling tonight. He should be focused on their father's demands, but all he could think about was Jace, out there with Clay, free in ways he could never be.

7

FOR MOTHER

C LAY

A Month Later

The call came late in the afternoon, just as the bar was starting to fill with the usual crowd. Clay was behind the bar counter, laughing with a couple of regulars when the phone rang. Clay answered. The voice on the other end was familiar—cold and detached like it always was. His father.

"Your mother's dead," his father said, without preamble. "Passed away two weeks ago. I mean to call, but...well, I forgot."

Clay's grip tightened on the phone, and his heart started to slam against his chest. He couldn't speak, couldn't breathe. Two weeks? Two goddamn weeks, and this was how he found out?

"And another thing," his father continued, as if he was discussing the weather. "We're broke. So, don't expect any more checks. The well's run dry."

Clay's vision went red. The world around him blurred as a rage flooded his veins, hot and all-consuming. His mouth before his mind could catch up. "I'm gonna kill you," he hissed into the phone. "I'm coming over right now. You're dead, old man."

His father's chuckle was low and dismissive. "By the time you get here, I'll be long gone. Good luck with whatever you think you're gonna do." The line went dead.

Clay stood there, the phone still pressed to his ear, trembling with fury. His mother was gone. The checks—his lifeline to his family—were gone. And his father...his father had always been an afterthought, a cold, distant figure who only reached out when it was convenient. But this? This was beyond anything Clay could tolerate.

He slammed the phone down on the counter and turned to Jace, who had walked over to him. The look in Jace's eyes said he knew something was very, very wrong.

"I need your help," Clay said, his voice shaking. "We're going to kill him."

Jace didn't ask questions. He didn't need to. He nodded, a quiet understanding passing between them. They'd been through hell and back up until now, and they were about to cross another line. One they couldn't uncross.

They left the bar and drove to his father's mansion, parking a couple blocks back, just out of sight. The sun was starting to set, casting long shadows across the sprawling estate. Clay's hands were shaking as they waited, the rage still boiling just beneath the surface.

Hours passed before they finally saw the headlights of his father's car pull out of the driveway. Clay's heart pounded in his ears as they followed him, the tension building with every mile. His father stopped at an ATM, and that's when Clay knew it was time.

His father out of the car, completely oblivious to the danger lurking behind him. Clay moved quickly, hopping off his bike, and pulling the wire from his jacket pocket as he crept up behind him. His father was no skinny man—this wasn't going to be easy. But Clay didn't care. He wanted him to suffer.

He looped the wire around his father's neck and pulled tight, but his father fought back, thrashing and kicking as Clay struggled to hold on. For a moment, Clay thought he might lose the battle, but then Jace was there, grabbing the wire with him, pulling tighter. They both grunted with effort, the wire digging into their hands, but they didn't stop. They couldn't.

It felt like an eternity, but finally, his father's body went limp. The fight drained out of him, and he collapsed to the ground. Clay's chest heaved, his breath coming in ragged gasps as the adrenaline surged through him. He stared down at his father's lifeless body, the reality of what he'd just done crashing down on him.

Tears welled up in his eyes, and before he could stop himself, they spilled over, rolling down his cheeks. He'd wanted this—he'd needed this—but now, standing over his dead father, he felt empty. Numb. He started to fall, his legs giving away beneath him, but Jace caught him, pulling him into a tight embrace.

"It's over," Jace whispered, holding him up as Clay's sobs wracked his body' "It's done."

Clay buried his face in Jace's shoulder, shaking uncontrollably. They stood there for what felt like forever, the weight of the moment pressing down on them both.

When they finally pulled away, the reality of what they'd done settled in. There was no going back. No undoing it. They left the body where it was, getting back on Clay's bike, and driving back to Velvet, neither of them saying a word.

Once inside, they headed straight to the bar, grabbing a bottle of whiskey and pouring glass after glass, trying to drown out the memory of what they'd just done. But no amount of alcohol could wash away the blood on their hands.

8

ROULETTE

JACE

A Day Later

Velvet was nearly empty when Cole strolled in. I was behind the bar cleaning up, trying to shake off the remnants of the night before. The weight of everything we'd been doing had started to sink in, gnawing at my insides. But when Cole entered, you couldn't show that. He sniffed out weakness like a shark to blood.

He didn't waste time on pleasantries. "Got a new job for you two," he said, tossing a couple of guns on the bar like it was nothing. Clay glanced over from his seat, already knowing we weren't going to like what came next.

"A rival," Cole said, lighting a cigarette and leaning back against the bar. "Took off with a pretty hefty stash of mine.

South LA. You'll know him when you see him. Drives a maroon Corvette with a big-ass hawk on the hood. Get it done quickly. Clean." He blew smoke in the air like he'd just ordered pizza and not a hit.

I took one of the guns in my hand, feeling its weight. I hated the way it felt now—like the physical embodiment of everything I'd become. Clay was already grabbing his jacket, too eager, too ready. "We'll find him," he'd said. "Won't take long."

We left Velvet, hooped on Clay's bike, and headed south, weaving through traffic toward the neighborhood we rarely ventured into. The streets felt different here, heavier. Clay rode with the same reckless abandon, leaving into curves like he didn't give a damn about whether we lived or died. I could feel that his father's death still was eating at him. Regardless, it wasn't like he was anywhere near ready to talk about it.

We circled the community centers Cole recommended we try before he left Velvet, eyes peeled for that telltale Corvette. It didn't take long. Parked outside a basketball court, shining under the hazy LA sun, was our target. The hawk on the hood made it obvious. Too obvious.

Clay revved the bike, pulling up alongside the car. I raised the gun, finger on the trigger, but my nerves got the best of me. I fired two shots, but neither of them hit. The rival's head snapped toward us, eyes wide, and in a flash, he was gunning it down the street.

"Fuck!" I yelled, watching the Corvette speed off. Clay grinned like this was the best part. "We'll get him," he said, pushing the bike to its limit. The chase was on, taking us from South LA, up past Inglewood, and eventually, winding toward Santa Monica. We were firing at the car, but he was slippery, weaving through traffic, and for a while, it felt like he might get away.

Clay, of course, wasn't in any rush. I could see the wild excitement in his eyes. He was enjoying the chase too much to end it early. It wasn't until we hit Hollywood that he finally aimed at something useful—the tires. The back tires of the Corvette exploded, sending the car spinning out of control. It barreled through a park, knocking down part of the fence, mulch flying everywhere, and finally crashed into a jungle gym, crushing the slide beneath its weight.

Clay's bike roared through the park and pulled up behind the car, and I got off, my gun heavy in my hand again. I walked toward the driver's window, adrenaline pushing me forward. The rival was slumped over the wheel, but I couldn't take chances. I aimed the gun, ready to pull the trigger.

The car's radio screamed out Michael Bolton's *Everybody's Crazy*. Looked like Bolton was the unofficial soundtrack of our lives now.

In time you'll learn what you don't understand, it's the human condition, it's the nature of man...

Before I could fire, a shot rang out. Pain seared through my arm as I stumbled back, clutching the wound. The bastard had fired first, catching me off guard.

Clay was on him in seconds, unloading his entire clip into the car, the shots ringing out across the empty park. The rival slumped over for good this time, blood splattering the inside of the cracked windshield.

"Shit, Jace!" Clay yelled, rushing over to me. He helped me to my feet, my arm hanging uselessly at my side. I gritted my teether against the pain. "Let's get the hell outta here," he said, pulling me back to the bike.

We made it back to Velvet in record time, Clay practically carrying me off the bike as I bled all over the floor. He was already on the phone with Cole, demanding the family doctor. "Jace's been shot," he said, voice shaking slightly. "Get the doctor here now."

When Cole arrived with the doctor, his expression was hard, unreadable. The doctor set to work immediately, patching me up, but Cole's cold stare was fixed on me the whole time. "You couldn't handle a simple task, could you?" he sneered. "Can't even shoot straight. Pathetic."

Clay shot him a look, stepping forward. "Back off, Cole."

Cole's hand moved faster than I expected, pulling a revolver from the front of his jeans and pointing it directly at Clay's chest. The room went deadly silent, the air thick with tension. Clay didn't back down, I smiled a little, but I could see the anger boiling inside him.

Cole had no emotion on his face, the revolver steady in his hand.

Clay clenched his fists, teeth grinding, but he stayed quiet.

No one moved.

No one spoke.

9

AN IDEA

C LAY

Later That Night

The whiskey burned as it slid down my throat, but it wasn't nearly enough to kill the fire still raging inside me. I laid back on Jace's bed, staring at the ceiling, the dim glow of the streetlights cutting through the thin curtains of his apartment. The air was thick with smoke from the cigarette we were passing between us, and I took a drag, feeling it fill my lungs before I handed it to him.

"Jace," I started, my voice tight. "We can't keep living like this. You know that, right?"

He grunted, his head turned away from me, eyes glazed from the alcohol. "What're you going on about now?"

"Cole," I said firmly, my eyes locked on him. "We have to

take him out. It's the only way. He's a liability, Jace. Dead weight. If we don't he's going to get us both killed."

He snorted, drunk and dismissive. "You've lost your damn mind. Kill Cole? That'll never happen. You know how he is. He'd see it coming from a mile away. And besides," he said, turning to look at me with bleary eyes, "he'd never hurt me. I'm his brother. Forget the idea, Clay. Just...forget it."

But I couldn't. The anger in my chest was too much to ignore. "I'm not forgetting it, Jace. If we don't make a move now, he's going to pull the trigger on us first. You saw the way he was today. He doesn't care about you like you think he does."

Jace shifted, taking a long drag from the cigarette, blowing the smoke out slowly. His face hardened, but there was something sad behind his eyes like the thought of betraying Cole was too much for him to handle. "No," he said, this time with more finality. "Cole's all I've got left. He won't do it. He won't kill me."

I wanted to scream, to shake him until he understood, but all the anger, all the frustration suddenly dissolved as he looked at me—those dark eyes, filled with years of pain and loyalty to the wrong people. My heart ached, and before I knew it, my fingers were tracing the lines of his face, and he leaned into my touch. The space between us, the tension that had been suffocating us both, broke in an instant.

Our lips met, the taste of whiskey and smoke mixing between us, and it wasn't long before the conversation was forgotten. The room felt smaller, the walls closing in as we gave in to each other, desperate to shed the weight of everything—the violence, the lies, the impossible decisions. For a few moments, we could escape it all, lose ourselves in something that felt pure, even amid all the chaos.

We made love, the kind that came from years of hurt

and desire. It was reckless, needy, and filled with the desperation of two people clinging to the only thing that still felt real in a world that had long since fallen apart. When it was over, we lay there, bodies entangled, breathing hard, and I pressed my head against him, whispering, "We can still get out of this. Together."

But Jace didn't respond. He just held me tighter, his silence telling me all I needed to know.

Unbeknownst to us, just outside the window, in a nondescript black van parked on the street, two men sat listening to everything that had transpired. A small blinking light on their equipment confirmed what they needed. One of them, sitting in the passenger seat, picked up a pager, his fingers working quickly over the buttons.

10

THE BREAK-UP

J ACE

Two Months Later

THE CLUB WAS RUNNING SMOOTHLY, money flowing in like the liquor we served every night. Velvet had become a home of sorts for Clay and me, but in the back of my mind, something was unraveling. Every day, every night spent tangled up with him in our apartments, loving each other as fiercely as we fought, I could feel the walls closing in. It wasn't Clay. It was Cole.

For months, Clay had been hounding me. "We have to do something about Cole," he'd say, time and time again. And each time, I'd shrug it off or change the subject. It wasn't that I didn't understand—hell, Clay was right. Cole was dangerous. His jobs were getting riskier, and his paranoia growing. But I couldn't sever that tie. The hold Cole had over me was too deep, too strong. He wasn't just my brother; he was my blood, my family. And no matter how much I loved Clay, I couldn't bring myself to imagine a world without Cole in it.

By the time Christmas rolled around, the tension between the three of us had hit a breaking point. Cole had been sniffing around, catching onto the undercurrents of Clay's plan, and his frustration with me for not stepping up. I'd seen the way Cole looked at us lately, with disdain and something else—something darker.

At my parents' house that night, the air was thick with expectation. The house was decked out in garlands, twinkling lights, and the kind of holiday cheer that only covered up the rot underneath. My parents had never been the sentimental type. They ran the family like a business—heartless, transactional, and efficient. And now, I was bringing Clay into the belly of the beast.

Dinner was laid out like a feast, turkey, ham, the works. Clay sat beside me, uneasy but trying to keep it together. He knew this wasn't just a dinner. It was a test. He had to show my parents that he was someone I could stand beside, someone worthy of their approval. And for a while, it seemed like we might just make it through.

But then Cole, always the sharpest knife in the drawer, decided to strike. He leaned back in his chair, a smug smile creeping across his face. "You know, Dad," he said casually, looking at our father but keeping his eye on me, "Jace's been fucking Clay for months now. He's gay. And weak. Not the man you raised him to be."

The words hung in the air like a curse. Clay's face went white, and my father's jaw clenched, his eyes narrowing at me with disappointment and disgust. Before anyone could react, Clay stood up so fast his chair scraped against the floor, the sound echoing through the room. He lunged at Cole, fists flying, the pent-up rage of months finally breaking free.

I watched in shock as they went at it, Cole's face taking blow after blow. Blood splattered across the whole tablecloth, and the sound of fists meeting flesh filled the room. Clay was stopping—he was breaking Cole down, piece by piece, and I couldn't move. I couldn't stop it. Part of me didn't want to.

It wasn't until my father pulled Clay off Cole, holding him back, that I realized what had happened. Cole's face was a mess, swollen and bloody, but his eyes were gleaming with satisfaction. He'd gotten exactly what he wanted. My father shoved Clay away, his voice venomous. "Get out. Leave this house and never come back. You're not welcome in this family."

Clay, panting and enraged, turned to me. His eyes, filled with anger and hurt, searched mine for a sign, for something—anything—that said I'd stand by him. But I knew what I had to do. I had no choice.

"Leave," I said. Clay's face twisted in disbelief, but I didn't stop. "Get the fuck out, Clay. You've done enough."

And then, as if to drive the knife deeper, I spat at his feet, the ultimate betrayal.

Clay's face broke—rage, sorrow, and betrayal all crashing over him at once. He stared at me, his eyes full of something I'd never be able to forget, then turned and stormed out of the house, slamming the front door behind him.

And just like that, he was gone.

. . .

THE SILENCE after Clay left was unbearable. My heart pounded in my chest as I stood there, frozen. My father turned to me, his face a cold mask of fury. The shame weighed down on me like a lead blanket, and I knew-whatever happened next would be the final blow.

"So, it's true," my father said, dripping with contempt. "You've been sneaking around, disgracing this family—lying to my face." He stepped closer, each word a dagger in my gut. "You've been fucking another man. A goddamn faggot, just like your brother."

I wanted to scream, to fight back, to tell him he was wrong about me, about Cole, about everything. But I was trapped in this nightmare. My body refused to move. I was paralyzed, just like I'd always been around him.

Before I could even react, my father grabbed me by the back of the neck and shoved me toward the dining table. The surface of the tablecloth pressed against my skin, and the blood from Cole's face was smeared across it, still warm. "You think you can live your life like this, huh?" he spat, forcing my face down into the mess. "You think you can humiliate me? In my house?"

I gasped as his hand yanked down my pants, exposing me to the room, to my mother, to Cole, who was starting to prop himself up against the wall. He brought his hand down on me—hard, sharp cracks that echoed in the room. The pain shot through me, but it was nothing compared to the humiliation. Each strike was a reminder of how powerless I was in front of him.

"I'll beat the fucking queer out of you I have to," he growled, more venom pouring from his lips. "You ever embarrass me again, you ever so much as look at another man, I'll kill you myself. Do you understand?"

I nodded, biting down on my lip so hard I could taste

blood. The tears blurred my vision, but I wouldn't let him see me break. Not completely.

Satisfied with his work, my father released me, leaving me slumped over the table, pants still down, sobbing in the splattered blood. He turned his attention to Cole, who had pulled himself up from the floor, barely conscious at this point after the beating Clay had given him.

Without hesitation, my father grabbed Cole by the collar, yanking him off the ground with savage strength. Cole's body went limp as he was slammed against the wall, the glass of our large family portrait shattering as his back hit it. The sound of the glass breaking was deafening, but it was nothing compared to the venom that continuously poured from our father's lips.

"You think you're any better, Cole?" he sneered, getting so close to his face I could see Cole's tears from across the room. "You think I don't know about your "tendencies"? You've been a coward your whole life, hiding behind your lies and your secrets. At least Jace—" He paused, a cruel smile curling on his lips. "At least Jace has the balls to be what he is. But you...you'll never be my son."

Cole's body crumpled under the weight of his words. His face was bloodied and bruised, but the real damage was deeper. I could see it, the way the light in his eyes dimmed, the way his spirit collapsed under the force of our father's cruelty.

Content with the destruction he'd caused, our father released Cole, letting him slide down the wall in a heap of broken glass. He stood there for a moment, towering over us both as if surveying his work. And then, without another word, he turned and stormed out of the dining room, the sound of his footfalls fading as he left us to drown in the wreckage of our family.

I stayed bent over the table, my body trembling, the pain throbbing through me in waves. I was nauseous. Cole sat slumped against the wall, his face buried in his hands, his sobs quiet but unrelenting. We were both broken, shattered by the man who was supposed to protect us, supposed to love us.

And then there was our mother, standing off to the side, her face pale and tear-streaked. She reached for a bottle of wine, her hands shaking as she poured herself a glass. She took a long sip, her lips trembling with each taste, her sobs barely audible between gulps.

She didn't say a word. She didn't comfort us, didn't try to fix the mess her husband made. She just stood there, drowning herself in her misery, as if it were all she knew how to do.

And there we were—Cole and I, the broken remnants of a family.

11

SECRETS REVEALED

CLAY

1986 - St. Patrick's Day - New York City

IT WAS the kind of cold that settled in your bones, even in March. New York had a way of making you feel both alive and numb at the same time. I'd been here for a few months now, tucked away in my condo on the Upper East Side, with Central Park right outside my window, a world apart from the chaos I left behind in Los Angeles. The bookstore I bought was my sanctuary, a quiet, steady rhythm compared to the violence and unpredictability of my former life.

Valentin had slipped into my life as easily as a breeze through an open window. He was different—soft in all the places I used to be hard, full of stories from his childhood in Italy, with a passion for food and wine that made me forget, at least for a while, the bitter taste of the past. We had been dating for three months now, and it felt right. Simple. Peaceful.

It was St. Patrick's Day, and the city was alive with energy. The streets were packed with people dressed in green, their laughter spilling out of pubs and restaurants. Valentin and I had joined the crowd for a bit, pub crawling our way through the Upper East Side, drinking pints of Guinness, and sharing quiet smiles between all the noise. But by the time midnight rolled around, we'd had enough of the crowds. We made our way back to my place, a little buzzed, our arms draped around each other as the city sparkled behind us.

"Let's make dinner," Valentin suggested once were back inside, his eyes lit up with excitement. "Something simple. Pasta. Wine. Maybe some garlic bread?" He smiled that day smile, the one that made me forget about everything else, if only for a little while.

I nodded, pulling him into the kitchen where we threw together a simple meal, laughing as we bumped into each other in passing. There was something intimate—domestic?—about it—the clinking of wine glasses, the smell of fresh garland olive oil, the sound of Valentin humming an old Italian song under his breath.

After dinner, we decided to play a few rounds of a board game. Something silly to close out the night before heading to bed. "Monopoly?" Valentin suggested, raising an eyebrow as he made his way to the closet. I could hear him rummaging through the shelves as I poured another glass of wine.

But then the rustling stopped. "Clay?" Valentin's voice was softer now, curious. I turned to see him standing next to me, holding a small dusty box. "What's this?"

My heart skipped a beat. I knew exactly what the box was. I hadn't opened it since I left Los Angeles. Inside were the remnants of a life I thought I buried—the photos of Jace and me, the journals I'd kept during those wild, painful years, and a few trinkets that meant more than I'd ever let on.

Valentin went to the living room and sat on the floor, pulling out the pictures, leafing through the journals with a look of fascination. "This is...you? In LA?" he asked, glancing up at me with wide eyes. "You look so different."

I could feel the weight of the past pressing down on me, the memoirs I tried so hard to escape crawling back to the surface. I wanted to brush it off, tell him it was nothing. I didn't want to lie to him. He didn't deserve that.

So, I sat down next to him and told him everything.

I TOLD HIM ABOUT JACE, about the love we had, about the clubs and the chaos, about the jobs we did for Cole, about how it all went wrong. How I'd run from it all, leaving behind the only person I'd ever truly loved. My voice cracked in places, but I kept going. I didn't leave anything out.

By the time I finished, Valentin was quiet, his hand resting gently on mine. His eyes, normally so bright and carefree, were serious now, filled with something that looked like understanding.

"I didn't know," he said softly, squeezing my hand. "I didn't know you carried all of this."

I swallowed, feeling the heaviness of everything I'd just shared, but also a strange sense of relief. "I thought I could leave it behind," I said, my voice barely above a whisper. "But it's still there, you know? All of it."

Valentin nodded, his fingers tracing the edge of one of the photos. "It's part of you," he said quietly. "And I love all of you."

VALENTIN

Two weeks had passed since Clay opened up to me about his past in Los Angeles. The photos, the journals, the story of Jace—it was all still fresh in my mind, but I didn't let it affect us. Or at least, I tried not to. We had something good here in New York, everything was working, and I wasn't about to let the ghost of some ex-lover ruin that.

I had a job to do, though. My cover job was in modeling and it had taken me back to LA for a few days—photo shoots, runway shows, the usual chaos. I told Clay I'd be back soon, kissed him on the cheek, and hopped on the next flight. He looked worried, but he trusted me, and I left knowing I'd see him again soon. I had work to do.

The shows went by in a blur of camera flashes and designer clothes, but it was that night at the Ritz-Carlton that everything shifted. I was sitting alone at a quiet corner table, picking at my meal, when Cole walked up, uninvited, and took the seat across from me. I hadn't seen him since I left Los Angeles. I wasn't particularly thrilled to see him now.

"So, how's our friend Clay?" Cole asked casually, his eyes gleaming with that sinister charm he always carried.

I didn't flinch. "He thinks he's moved on," I replied, trying to sound indifferent. "He's happy. He doesn't talk about Jace anymore. He's focused on his bookstore, his life in New York."

Cole leaned back in his chair, laughing softly. "He thinks he's free, doesn't he? Well, we both know better, don't we?"

I met his gaze, not responding. I knew exactly what Cole meant. Clay might think he's escaped his past, but that wasn't how things worked. Especially not with Cole.

"I trust you'll take care of it," Cole said, his voice dead serious. "Don't forget why you're in his life, Valentin. Your past...in the Italian military...should make this easy for you."

I felt a chill run down my spine, but I didn't let it show. Cole was right. My past was complicated, and I owed him. This was all part of the deal, and I had to see it through, no matter how much it made my stomach turn. Clay had no idea who I was.

I watched Cole leave the restaurant, his dark figure disappearing into the hotel. I didn't have much time left. Clay trusted me, and now I had to betray that trust. I didn't have a choice.

COLE

Back in my suite, I found Jace exactly where I'd left him—lying on the bed, staring blankly at the ceiling, lost in whatever pit of despair he'd crawled into. Beside him sat the older man, a "guest" I'd arranged for the evening. He was already in the middle of it, taking his time like it was some sick ritual.

I closed the door softly, watching them from across the room. Jace didn't move, didn't speak. He never did during these "sessions." He'd learned a long time ago what was expected of him, and by now, he complied without resistance.

The man grunted, oblivious to my presence as he carried on, and I poured myself a drink from the bar. I sipped it slowly, leaning against the window, watching the city lights flicker outside. This had become our tradition, our sick way of keeping Jace in check, making sure he remembered his place.

"Remember, Jace," I murmured to myself, though I knew he could hear me. "You'll never be free. No matter what Clay thinks, no matter what plans you have...you're mine. Always."

I smirked, swirling the ice in my glass, and listening to the sounds from the bed. Soon enough, I'd deal with Clay too. They both thought they could escape, but no one escaped me. Not without paying a price.

JACE

The humiliation was unbearable, but I didn't cry anymore. I had learned long ago that tears didn't help. They just made Cole feel more powerful. So I lay there, motionless, waiting for it to be over. The older man, whoever he was, grunted and sweated over me, completely lost to anything but his pleasure.

But in my head, I wasn't here. I was with Clay, in the quiet moments before everything fell apart, when we were lying in bed, after Clay initially brought up his "idea," plotting our future. Clay had no awareness of Cole's real control over me, not fully. But he would soon.

We had a plan, Clay and I. And it was only a matter of time before everything came together. Cole thought he had the upper hand, that I was too weak to fight back. But he didn't know the full story. Clay and I had been working on this for months. We were going to take him down.

But convincing myself of this plan, convincing myself I was strong enough to pull it off, was the hardest part. Every day, I had to wear a mask, make it seem like I was still Cole's broken little puppet. But deep down, I was fighting to reclaim my life. The worst part was lying to Clay. I had to make him believe I was still under Cole's thumb, even when I wasn't sure I had the strength to break free. I lied to Cole to survive, lied to myself to endure, and lied to Clay to keep him safe. It doesn't make sense when I say it out loud but I knew what I was doing. It took everything in me not to crumble.

I closed my eyes, tuning out the world, and pictured Clay's face. It was the only thing that kept me going, the only thing that gave me the strength to endure this nightmare.

Soon, I told myself.
Soon we'll be free.

12

WINE, WINE, WINE

C LAY

THREE DAYS Later

THE NIGHT HAD STARTED SO PERFECTLY. I'd just left the grocery store, arms full of dinner supplies, a fresh bottle of Pinot Noir, and a bouquet of roses nestled in the crook of my arm. Tonight was special. Valentin was supposed to be back, and I wanted to welcome him home in a way that felt like is—warm, intimate, simple.

I hummed as I walked back to the condo, the city's energy swirling around me, but I was calm. I had Michael Bolton on my mind, already hearing his soulful voice in the background of our night. By the time I got home, I set to work, chopping vegetables, searing the steak, and pouring two glasses of wine as the smell of garlic and rosemary filled the condo. The record player spun softly in the living room, Bolton's voice raspy, smooth, and familiar as I set the table with care. Everything was ready. Now, I just had to wait for Valentin.

But as minutes ticked by, and then an hour, my nerves started to kick in. I glanced at the clock. He should've been here by now. I checked my watch, pushing down the sudden knot of anxiety in my chest. Maybe he was just running late. I walked to the phone in the kitchen and dialed the airport, hoping for an easy answer. His flight had landed hours ago I was told.

That's when I heard it—a soft creak from the bedroom, just faint enough to make me pause. Michael Bolton's *Fool's Game* filled the air, but underneath it, something else lurked. "Valentin?" I called, but the only response was Bolton's voice over the record.

I moved to the bedroom slowly, eventually standing in the doorway, my heart racing. It was dark, nothing out of place. "Valentin?" I called again, my voice now tight with confusion. Still nothing. I turned, ready to search elsewhere, and that's when I felt it—a sharp, searing pain in my shoulder.

I staggered, gasping as the kitchen knife pierced my skin. Valentin was behind me, his face something wild and unrecognizable as he climbed onto my back, trying to pull me down. Instinct kicked in, and through the pain, I fought my way to the kitchen, slamming him against the fridge with all the force I could muster at the moment. He tumbled off me, the knife still lodged in my shoulder, and I yanked it out, adrenaline coursing through me.

Valentin recovers quickly, shoving me into the wall beneath the phone I'd just used to call the airport. The receiver clattered to the floor, and without thinking, I grabbed it, wrapping the curly cord around his throat, trying to stop him. But Valentin wasn't done. He slashed at the cord with the knife, cutting it loose, but nicking his neck in the process, a thin red line of blood appearing like a twisted smile.

We crashed into the dining table after we scrambled to our feet, both of us going down hard as the wood buckled and collapsed beneath our weight. The sound was deafening, but over it all, Michael Bolton's voice climbed, the intensity of the song building as if it were narrating the madness. My hands scrambled for something, anything, and then they found the wine bottle.

I swung it hard. The glass shattered against Valentin's skull, the sound mixing with Bolton's fading song as the blood sprayed everywhere, splattering across the remnants of the dinner I had so carefully prepared. Valentin's body twitched and then went still, crumpling beneath me.

I stood up, panting, the broken bottle still clutched in my hand as I looked down at the man I'd spent months building a life with. Blood soaked into the hardwood floor, and into my clothes, and yet the only thing I could hear now was the silence that followed the end of the record. Bolton's voice had stopped. The music is gone.

And so was Valentin.

THE MESS HAD BEEN OVERWHELMING at first. Blood stained the hardwood floor and splattered across the white walls. The weight of the body had felt unnatural as I dragged it to the closet, limbs heavy, lifeless. I wasn't new to this. The year before in Los Angeles had taught me enough, but this...this felt different. The cleaner arrived within an hour—quiet, fast, no questions asked. He wiped away the evidence, took the body discreetly, and eventually left the place as pristine as it had been before the chaos broke loose.

The cleaner even patched up my wound. Gave me stitches. I drank some whiskey.

Once everything was spotless, I collapsed onto the couch, sinking into the soft cushions. The room was quiet again, but inside my head, everything was loud. I couldn't shake the feeling that this was somehow connected to Jace. Or worse, Cole. Maybe both. My mind raced through the possibilities—was this a warning? A message? Had Jace sent him? But why? The plan we had cooked up to take down Cole was still that—a plan. We hadn't moved on it yet. So what was this? A reminder? A threat? My chest tightened as I realized it could have easily gone the other way. It could've been me lying in a pool of blood.

I rubbed my temples, trying to steady my breathing. Every scenario pointed back to one thing—I had to get out of New York. This was just the beginning. The feeling in my gut, the one that never steered me wrong, usually, told me that there was more coming. This was the start of something bigger, something I couldn't outrun this time.

I headed back to the bedroom and grabbed a duffle bag from the closet, stuffing it with clothes—enough for a week, maybe more. My hands were shaking as I packed, thoughts spiraling into a dark place. Jace had to be involved, even if indirectly. Maybe he wanted me back in LA. Either way, I couldn't stay here. Not anymore.

New York wasn't safe.

Valentin...well, I didn't even know how to think about him.

As I zipped up the bad and threw it over my shoulder, careful not to reopen my wound, a wave of nausea hit me. The last time I felt this sick, this cornered, I'd been on a job for Cole, standing outside some crooked politician's office, about to plant evidence to destroy his career. I couldn't believe I was back in this life, back in the same web of lies and violence.

I took a deep breath and headed out the door, leaving the pristine condo behind. There was no turning back now. The city buzzed with life around me, truly the city that never sleeps, but all I could hear was the pounding of my heart in my chest. The taxi ride to the airport was a blur. The driver's small talk washed over me, his voice blending into the hum of the city. My mind was locked on one thing —Los Angeles.

I had to confront Jace. I had to get answers. If Cole was pulling strings, if this was some twisted game to him, I needed to know where Jace truly stood with me. After everything we've been through, after the love we shared, how could he send someone to kill me? Or worse, let Cole do it for him?

The plane tickets felt heavy in my hands as I stood in line at the airport. My pulse quickened. LA was just a few hours away, and with it, the life I thought I'd left behind for good. There was no telling what I'd find when I got there, but one thing was certain: this wasn't over.

The last thought I had before boarding the plane was of Jace's face, the last time I saw him, sitting at me as I was thrown out of his family's Christmas dinner. I clenched my fists. This time, I wouldn't be so easily dismissed.

13

LOOSE ENDS

COLE

NEXT DAY

THE POKER GAME in Silverlake was going well, Cole mused. He had won a few hands and lost a few, but the whiskey kept flowing, and the night was still young. His men surrounded the table, faces dimly lit by the low-hanging bulbs overhead, smoke curling up toward the ceiling like a sinister fog. Cole's eyes scanned the cards in his hand, masking the frustration simmering underneath. His mind wasn't on the game tonight. Too many loose ends—Jace, Clay, the business.

Just as he was about to place his bet, one of his men, Marco, hurried into the bar. The moment Cole saw the look on his face, he knew. Marco leaned down, whispering in

Cole's ear, "It's Valentin. Either dead or gone. Clay's work, most likely. One of our guys working with Valentin found their condo empty. A little too clean."

Cole's pulse quickened, but his face remained stone-cold. Dead. It had to be. Valentin wasn't the kind to just vanish. Valentin owed Cole. Clay had finally started to push back, to figure out the deeper game Cole had been playing all along. A slow smile crept across Cole's face. Clay had balls; he'd give him that. But this was a problem Cole couldn't afford to ignore.

Dismissing his hand with a flick of his wrist, Cole stood up, tossing his cards face up on the table. "I'm out," he said to the other players, not bothering to explain. His mind was racing now. Clay was coming for him—that much was clear. And if Clay was bold enough to kill Valentin, he had to assume Jace was involved, too. He cursed under his breath. The idea of Jace and Clay working together made his skin crawl. That was not a betrayal he could let slide.

Cole drove through the narrow, winding streets of Silverlake, his jaw clenched in silent fury. By the time he reached Jace's apartment, his patience had run thin. He stormed up the stairs and banged on the door, not waiting for an answer before kicking it open. Jace was sitting on the couch, looking stunned. Cole's eyes bore into him, and without a word, he yanked his brother up by the collar.

"What the fuck are you doing, Cole?" Jace sputtered, trying to shove him away.

Cole didn't bother with an explanation. Instead, he dragged Jace out of the apartment and into his car. Jace struggled, shouting, throwing punches that Cole easily deflected. But Cole wasn't in the mood to fight—at least, not yet. He had to get his brother somewhere private, somewhere quiet.

. . .

They sped through the streets of Downtown LA, the city's neon lights reflecting off the windshield. Jace's protests fell on deaf ears. Cole didn't say a word as they pulled up to an old, abandoned warehouse, hidden between blocks of decaying buildings. It was a place Cole had used before—a place where questions were answered, one way or another.

The moment they entered the warehouse, Jace tried to make a run for it. Cole caught him easily, slamming him against a post before tying him to a rusted chair. Jace was still cursing, still trying to fight back, but Cole's grip was too strong. His younger brother was always the rebellious type, but Cole knew how to handle him.

"Enough!" Cole barked, his voice as dangerous as ever. "You're going to tell me what's going on. I know Clay's in town, and my associate, Valentin, is dead."

Jace's face paled, but he kept his mouth shut, glaring up at Cole with defiance in his eyes. Cole chuckled, shaking his head. He walked over to a metal shelf in the corner of the room, where a few tools and supplies were scattered. He picked up a bucket and a rag, his fingers tightening around the handle.

"You're going to tell me everything, Jace," Cole said. "Because if you don't, I'm going to find out anyway. And trust me, you don't want to make this any harder than it has to be."

Jace didn't respond. His eyes followed Cole as he filled the bucket with water from an old faucet, the steady drip-drip of the water echoing in the space. Cole's smile returned, cruel and cold.

. . .

JACE

TIED TO THE RUSTED CHAIR, he knows this could be it. Cole is going to kill him. And Clay? He's in town? He must have remembered their plan. And this Valentin? Who is that?

Cole walks over to Jace, grips his head to hold it in place, places the rag on his face, and pours the water on top. Jace can taste the rusty water as he begins to choke and gasp for air. His lungs scream for oxygen, and his mind races. Clay. His thought before he dies will be Clay. Jace shakes violently against his duct tape restraints on the chair but to no avail. The tape digs deeper into his wrists and ankles, burning his skin as he thrashes.

Cole stops and removes the rag, calmly walking to refill the water, his steps slow, deliberate. He turns his head slightly toward Jace, "What's going on, Jace? What are you and Clay planning?"

Jace stays silent, gasping for air. He can feel the weight of Cole's growing impatience like a knife at his throat.

Cole returns, rag and water in hand. "I'll ask again. What's the plan?" Before Jace can form a thought, the rag is back on his face, and water pours, soaking into his mouth, and his nose. The suffocation is immediate, his body screaming as it tries to fight off the instinctual pain that floods his veins. The world is dark at the edges, his consciousness slipping as he gags and coughs.

It feels like an eternity before Cole pulls the rag away again. Jace gasps desperately, each breath burning as the air fills his waterlogged lungs. Cole grips the back of the chair and leans close, his breath hot against his face. "Tell me what I want to know, or we'll keep this up all night. What are you and Clay up to?"

Jace's head swims, but he knows a third rough might kill him. He can't hold out anymore. His body is broken, and his mind is fogged from the pain. "We were going to kill you," Jace spits out. His words come out in a hoarse whisper. "You've lost it, Cole. You're insane. It's not my fault you can't face who you are. And our family?" He laughs bitterly. "Fuck them. Family isn't everything."

Cole's eyes flare with fury. He reaches for the water again, prepared to drown him one more time. But Jace sees it coming. With everything left in him, he surges forward, smashing his head into Cole's face. The impact sends Cole reeling, his grip on the chair loosening. In a blind scramble, Jace rocks the chair back and forth, feeling the rusty metal groan beneath his weight. It gives. The legs snap, and he crashes to the ground, the brittle rust slicing through the tape around his ankles. He grips the armrests off the chair and yanks, both breaking off instantly and using them to cut the rest of the tape off.

Cole sitting up from the floor, blood streaming from his nose. Before he can react, Jace kicks him hard in the gut, once, twice, enough to knock the air out of his lungs. Jace doesn't wait to see the damage. He's running, heart pounding, searching for the nearest exit. He bursts through the warehouse doors and spots Cole's car parked haphazardly out front.

Without a second thought, Jace dives through the open passenger window, pulling himself into the driver's seat. His hands fumble for the keys. Nothing. "Fuck." He scans the dashboard, his fingers shaking as he hot-wires the car. The engine roars to life just as he sees Cole stumbling toward the exit in the rearview mirror.

Jace slams his foot on the gas and speeds off, his mind racing faster than the car. He has to find Clay.

Where would he be?

14

CONFESSIONS

J ACE

Earlier - Same Day

Jace sat at his typewriter, the familiar clack of the keys echoing through his quiet apartment. His fingers moved quickly, the words flowing onto the page like blood spilling from an open wound. His hands shook, not from fear, but from the weight of everything he'd carried for so long. Every lie, every betrayal, every sin that had built this life he no longer recognized. The truth was, he knew it was over. He could feel it deep in his gut—the suffocating heaviness that had been with him since that last night at Velvet. Something was coming, and this time, there was no escape.

He paused, staring at the half-filled page before him. His heart pounded in his chest, and the cold sweat that lined his skin made him shiver despite the heat in the room. This letter—this confession—was all he had left. His one final attempt to be honest, to purge the poison that had infected every corner of his life. If this was his last day, as he feared it might be, then someone had to know. Someone had to understand why it all went to hell.

Jace started typing again, his thoughts pouring out in raw, jagged sentences. He wrote about his family—the drug empire that had consumed them, how Cole had become a monster under their father's thumb, and how he, Jace, had failed to stop any of it. He admitted to his guilt, his cowardice in staying silent, in letting Cole take control while he stood by, watching as the family fell deeper into darkness.

He wrote about their father—his cruelty, his twisted idea of what it meant to be a man. Jace could still feel the sting of his father's hand, the humiliating punishment he had endured that Christmas night, bent over the dinner table like a child. It was all there, in brutal, honest detail. Every shame, every moment of weakness. He didn't hold back. There was no point anymore.

But as the typewriter clicked on, the tone of the letter shifted. Jace's fingers slowed as he began to write about Clay. His breath hitched in his throat as he tried to find the right words. How could he put into words what Clay meant to him? The only person who had ever truly seen him—not Jace the Renwick son, or the reluctant heir to a drug empire —but just Jace. The man. The one who wanted to be more than what his family had forced him to be.

He typed slowly now, each keystroke deliberate. He wrote about the nights they spent at Velvet, the way Clay had made him laugh, the way they had danced together like no one was watching, how they'd made love like it was their last chance. He confessed his love for Clay—the only real thing he had left. The only thing that had made sense in the chaos of his life.

Jace's hands trembled as he finished the final lines. He admitted how much Clay had saved him in ways he didn't think were possible, even as he knew their love had been built on broken foundations. He'd been too scared to leave Cole behind, too scared to leave the only life he'd ever known, but Clay had given him a glimpse of freedom—a freedom he might never truly have.

He sat back in his chair, staring at the letter. It was done. Everything was out in the open. No more lies. No more secrets. If someone found this after he was gone, they would know the truth. They would know what happened between him and Cole, between him and Clay. And maybe, just maybe, they would understand.

The dark feeling in his gut only deepened as he folded the letter carefully and placed it in an envelope. He scrawled Clay's name on the front, his heart aching as he sealed it shut. It felt final. Too final.

Jace lit a cigarette, taking a long drag as he stared at the envelope sitting on the table. There was nothing more to say. No more words to write. All he could do now was wait. Wait for the inevitable, for whatever was coming next. He exhaled, watching the smoke curl up toward the ceiling, and for the first time in a long time, he felt something close to peace.

But even as the calm settled over him, the fear lingered in the back of his mind. Was this truly the end? Would this letter be the last thing he left behind? Jace didn't know. All he knew was that the shadows were closing in, and there was nothing left to do but face them.

15

FEELS LIKE THIS

J ACE'S MOTHER

Earlier - Same Day

The master bedroom was dimly lit, a single lamp casting a soft, amber glow across the room. Jace's mother, frail and pale, sat on the edge of the bed, nursing a half-empty bottle of wine, her fingers trembling with the weight of a decision she had been contemplating for weeks. The bitter taste of cheap red wine was a comfort now, numbing the sharp edges of her thoughts as she stared blankly at the reflection in the vanity mirror. Behind her, swaying ever so slightly in the draft, was the noose, suspended from the ceiling fan, casting a long, haunting shadow across the room.

She was hollowed out—years of living under the oppressive hand of her husband had drained her of everything.

What was left was a shell, a woman who had watched her family fall apart, unable to intervene. She had lost her voice, her will, and her sense of purpose long ago, trapped in a marriage that was suffocating, toxic, and inescapable. The man she had married had become a monster over time, a figure who controlled not only her life but the lives of their sons, Jace and Cole. She was complicit in their suffering by doing nothing. By being nothing.

The wine warmed her as it slid down her throat, and she took another deep gulp, her eyes settling on the noose again. How many times had she thought about this? Ending it. It was always there, lingering in the back of her mind, like a distant whisper, a seduction she couldn't resist any longer. The family was over, shattered beyond repair. There was no redemption left. No saving them. She'd failed her children. And for that, there was only one escape.

Her body was thin, almost translucent under the soft glow of the light, her veins visible beneath the fragile surface of her skin. She ran her hand over her bony wrist, feeling the pulse of life there, weak but steady. Soon, it would stop, and maybe, just maybe, the silence that followed would bring peace. Maybe then, she wouldn't have to hear the screams, the violence, the hatred that had filled this house for so many years. The silence seemed like the only thing that could set her free.

She drained the rest of the wine, letting the bottle slip from her fingers and roll across the floor with a dull thud. Slowly, she climbed onto the bed, her knees sinking into the soft mattress as she reached for the noose. Her fingers trembled as she slipped the rope around her neck, the rough fibers scratching at her skin. It was tight, too tight, but she didn't adjust it. It felt right, like the weight of everything pulling her down all at once.

She glanced at the note on the dresser, the simple words written in her neat, delicate handwriting: *What does family mean?* The question haunted her, gnawing at the edge of her consciousness. Was it love? Was it duty? Was it pain? She didn't know anymore. The family she had wanted, dissolved into a nightmare. Her husband had seen to that. He had destroyed them, and now, she was following the destruction to its conclusion.

It was surreal, this moment, the point of no return. A deep part of her wanted to fight it, wanted to rip the noose from her neck and scream at the injustice of it all. But she was too tired. Too broken. She'd been fighting for too long, even if only in silence, and she had nothing left to give.

She thought about Jace. She thought about Cole. Her boys. They were lost, tangled in the web of their father's legacy. She couldn't save them, couldn't protect them from what was coming. She could only hope that, in time, they would find a way out that didn't lead them here, to the same place she had arrived at. But she doubted it. This family was poison, and it had seeped into every fiber of their lives.

With one last, deep breath, she braced herself for the inevitable pull, for the final surrender. The room around her seemed to darken, and she closed her eyes, imagining, just for a second, what peace might feel like. She let her body lean forward, into the rope, into the release.

In the hallway, there was a sudden sound—the door creaking open, footsteps approaching. Her heart skipped a beat, panic flooding her veins.

STANDING THERE, framed by the dim light of the lamp, was her husband. His broad, looming figure cast a long shadow over the room, a figure she had once loved, now only a symbol of everything that had gone wrong.

He stood there, silent, his eyes scanning the scene—his wife kneeling on the bed, the noose around her neck, the note on the dresser. He didn't move, didn't react. It was as though this moment meant nothing to him, just another inconvenience in his tightly controlled world. She could feel his coldness from across the room, a chill that seeped into her bones.

Her voice, trembling and small, broke the silence. "Do you love me?" It was a desperate plea, a final attempt to understand the man she had shared her life with. She wanted to believe that somewhere, buried deep within him, there was still a fragment of the man she had fallen in love with. But the years had worn her down, and now, all she needed was one honest answer.

He stared at her, his eyes hard, calculating, as if weighing whether to bother responding at all. The seconds dragged on, and for a moment, she thought he might walk away without saying a word. But then, he shook his head, slowly, deliberately, confirming what she had known all along but had been too afraid to fully accept.

Her breath caught in her throat as his answer hit her like a final blow. A tear rolled down her cheek, hot and bitter, as her chest tightened with the weight of everything she had lost. She had hoped for so long that there might be something that could be salvaged. But there was nothing. There had never been anything.

Without a word, he turned and walked away, leaving the door open behind him, the cold draft from the hallway creeping into the room like the final chill of death. His footsteps faded down the corridor, echoing in the silence, and the house felt emptier than it had before.

She let more tears fall, her body shaking with quiet sobs as the last remnants of hope dissolved into the air around her. There was no going back. There was no saving what was left. She closed her eyes, her mind a blur of memories, of love lost and promises broken. She leaned further, surrendering to the pull of the noose, and with one last, quiet breath, she gave in.

16

ROLL WITH IT

Cole

Present

Cole's hands gripped the steering wheel, knuckles white from the force. He could still feel the sting in his chest—the rage bubbling just beneath the surface, threatening to tear him apart. His eyes narrowed as he tailed Jace, watching the rear lights of his brother's car flicker through the darkness. The streets blurred past them, a chaotic mix of neon and shadows, as they weaved through Downtown Los Angeles. Cole's pulse thudded in his ears, drowning out everything except the engine's roar and the growing urge to end this.

He reached for the revolver on the passenger seat, feeling its cold weight against his palm. He raised it, aiming for Jace's tires, but the shot was a gamble. Jace was smart, too smart. Every time Cole thought he had him pinned, Jace would swerve at the last second, dodging obstacles like he'd been planning this route for years. People screamed and jumped out of the way as they sped through crowded intersections, but Cole didn't care. He was beyond caring about civilians, about the damage they were leaving in their wake. He was only focused on Jace—and what he had to do.

The car chase dragged them from DTLA into Hollywood, past clubs, movie theaters, and busy restaurants. Cole tried to outmaneuver Jace, pressing the gas harder, attempting to cut him off at every turn, but Jace was relentless. His brother always had a knack for getting out of tight spots, but this was different. Cole could feel it. This wasn't just about outsmarting him—this was personal.

He squeezed the trigger again, aiming low this time. The bullet pinged off the side of Jace's car, just missing the back wheel. Cole swore under his breath, gripping the wheel tighter as Jace veered onto the sidewalk, barely missing a group of pedestrians. Traffic was a nightmare, and it was only getting worse as they neared West Hollywood.

West Hollywood, Cole thought bitterly. Of course. He knew where Jace was headed. Velvet. The club. Clay. It all made sense now.

Cole's jaw clenched as the realization hit him. Clay was involved in this—he had to be. Jace wouldn't be running like this if he didn't have someone to protect, someone to run to. The pieces fell into place in Cole's mind, and the fire inside him burned hotter. He was going to end this, one way or another.

They turned another corner, the glitzy lights of West Hollywood's nightlife flickering around them as Cole struggled to keep up. He could see Velvet in the distance now, its neon sign glowing like a beacon. Jace was getting desperate.

The streets were too tight for the kind of driving they were doing, and it was only a matter of time before someone made a mistake.

Cole slammed his foot on the gas, determined to close the gap. He fired another shot, this time aiming higher, hoping to shatter Jace's rear window. The glass exploded in a shower of shards, but Jace didn't slow down. If anything, he sped up, dodging between parked cars and into the alleyways that lined the streets of West Hollywood.

Cole cursed again, trying to keep his focus as Jace led him deeper into the heart of the city. He could feel his frustration mounting with every passing second, the weight of his father's expectations pressing down on him like a vice. He couldn't fail now. Not after everything.

As they tore through the narrow streets, Cole's mind raced. He couldn't let this continue. He wouldn't let Jace ruin what little control he had left. He had to stop him—before it was too late. The thought of Clay waiting at Velvet, maybe even expecting Jace to show up any minute, made Cole's blood boil. Clay had always been a thorn in his side, a distraction for Jace. And now, he was part of the problem, a loose end that needed tying up.

The car chase finally spilled into the street outside Velvet, the club's familiar façade looming over them. Jace's car screeched to a halt near the entrance, and before Cole could even think, Jace was out of the car and running toward the alley next to the building. Cole didn't hesitate. He slammed on the brakes, abandoning his car and sprinting after Jace.

The alley was narrow, lined with dumpsters and brick walls, and it reeked of piss and garbage. Cole's boots pounded against the pavement as he closed the distance between them. Jace was fast, but Cole had the advantage of anger and sheer determination driving him forward.

"Jace!" Cole yelled, his voice echoing off the walls as he raised his revolver, aiming squarely at his brother's back.

Jace skidded to a stop, breathing hard, but he didn't turn around. His shoulders tensed, and for a moment, Cole thought he might listen. But then Jace took off again, darting further into the alley, deeper into the shadows.

Cole fired. The shot rang out in the tight space, reverberating through the alley. He missed by inches as Jace ducked behind a stack of crates, taking cover. Cole swore under his breath and moved in closer, his grip tightening on the gun.

He approached cautiously, stepping over broken glass and trash, his eyes scanning the darkness for any sign of movement. He knew Jace was still there, hiding just out of sight. But for how long? Cole's heartbeat pounded in his ears, his breath coming in short, sharp bursts as he prepared for whatever came next.

And then he heard it. Footsteps—behind him.

Cole whipped around, gun raised, but it was too late. A figure emerged from the shadows, grabbing him from behind, andpinning his arms to his sides.

Cole's heart thudded in his chest, every beat echoing in his ears like a drum of finality. He wasn't ready for this to be the end. His pulse quickened as the officer reached for his cuffs. Panic surged through Cole's veins, the instinct to survive, to fight, rising like wildfire.

As the cold metal of the cuffs touched his wrist, he twisted violently, using every ounce of strength to break free. The cop struggled to maintain control, but Cole was quicker. In a desperate move, he pulled out his revolver, the familiar weight grounding him for a second before he emptied it into the officer's chest. The sound of each shot rang out, deafening in the narrow alley. The officer's body slumped to the ground, lifeless, blood pooling on the cracked pavement beneath him.

Cole stood there for a moment, breathing hard, the smoke from his gun lingering in the cold night air. His mind raced. He couldn't let this be the end—not like this. Without another thought, he sprinted toward the end of the alley, feet pounding against the ground as he ran for the back door of the Velvet. The door was wide open.

STEPPING INSIDE, Cole moved slowly, his eyes scanning the shadows. The club was empty, just remnants of the night's chaos left behind—half-empty glasses, overturned stools, and the lingering scent of smoke. He moved cautiously past the bar, then toward the hallway leading to the back offices, the sound of something slamming breaking through the silence.

His pulse quickened again, this time with a different kind of adrenaline. He crept down the hallway, his hand hovering over his side where he wished another gun would be. The door at the end was slightly ajar. He could hear rustling, the scrape of something heavy being shifted. With a final breath, Cole pushed the door open, bursting into the room.

Jace was there, standing by the desk, his face twisted in anger and something else—fear, maybe. In his hands, he gripped the landline phone, the cord swinging loosely. Before Cole could react, Jace swung it toward him with everything he had. The heavy base of the phone crashed into Cole's head, sending him reeling backward. The force knocked him into the wall, pain exploding through his skull. He slumped, blood trickling down his face, his vision swimming with black spots.

Through the haze of pain, Cole barely registered the sound of Jace's footsteps as he fled. The front door slammed shut in the distance, followed by the unmistakable screech of tires tearing out of the parking lot.

Gritting his teeth against the pain, Cole reached up and felt the warm stickiness of his blood on his forehead. His breath came in shallow gasps, but he wasn't done yet. Not by a long shot. With a shaking hand, he grabbed the phone that had been used to knock him down, pressing the redial button.

The line rang once, twice, before a familiar voice clicked on—the voice he was expecting. Clay's answering machine.

"Leave a message."

Cole smirked through the pain. He knew exactly where he was headed next.

COLE'S HANDS were trembling as he gripped the steering wheel, his knuckles white as he sped through the streets of Los Angeles. The adrenaline was burning in his veins, his breath coming in ragged bursts. He could still feel the thud from when he smashed into that cop car as he left Velvet, the sickening sound of metal against metal echoing in his mind. It was over. The façade was cracking. There was no coming back from this.

The city blurred around him, neon lights and blurred faces passing by like ghosts. The rage that simmered beneath his skin was boiling over now. He could feel it in his chest, his heart pounding against his ribs, his mind racing with a thousand thoughts, none of them making any sense.

All he could focus on was the singular, brutal truth: Jace had betrayed him. And Clay—Clay had corrupted him.

He couldn't let this stand. He had nothing left to lose. Not after tonight. Cole wiped the sweat from his brow with the back of his hand, trying to steady himself. The shotgun. It was in the trunk. It had been there for months, waiting for something—some moment that he never thought would come, but now here it was. His path was clear.

The streets of East Hollywood were dark and quiet as he pulled up in front of Clay's building, the familiar ache in his gut returning as he saw Jace's car parked out front. He felt a strange sort of calm wash over him as he killed the engine and stepped out of the car. This was it. His final act.

He walked around to the trunk, popping it open and pulling out the shotgun, the cold metal heavy in his hands. The weight was grounding. This was power. This was control. He slammed the trunk shut, his breath forming clouds in the cool night air as he stared up at the apartment building. He knew this place. He'd been here before, not that long ago, when things were different. When things still made sense.

Now, none of it made sense. Jace, Clay—it was all falling apart. The years of loyalty he'd given, the sacrifices—meaningless. They had turned on him, plotting behind his back. He had seen it in Jace's eyes, the hesitation, the doubt. It all led to this.

Cole climbed the stairs two at a time, his grip tightening on the shotgun with each step, the echo of his footsteps ringing in his ears. He wasn't going to think about what came next. He wasn't going to let the guilt or fear or anything else stop him. He couldn't.

When he reached the door to Clay's apartment, he stood still for a moment, just listening. He heard Jace and Clay yelling. There was a calm before the storm, a stillness that made his skin prickle. He could feel the anger bubbling back up, threatening to spill over again. With a growl, he lifted his boot and kicked the door in, the wood splintering as it gave way under the force.

17

RECYCLING

COLE'S FATHER

Earlier - Same Day

THE OLD MAN walked down the grand staircase of his mansion, each step heavy with the weight of years spent chasing ghosts. His wife's sobs had finally quieted, the sound now replaced by the eerie silence of a house too large, too empty. He had seen that look in her eyes before, the deadness. It had been there for years now, ever since they lost control—over the family, over the boys, over themselves.

As he moved through the dimly lit kitchen, his fingers brushed absentmindedly against the cold marble countertops. He couldn't remember the last time he had sat in this kitchen for an actual meal, or spoken to either of his sons without venom lacing his voice. Jace. Cole. Their names echoed in his head, their faces burned into his mind. He had tried so hard to shape them, mold them into something resembling the men they were supposed to be. But they had slipped through his fingers, just like his own life had.

Outside, the warm evening air greeted him as he stepped through the sliding glass doors onto the patio. The pool glistened under the soft glow of the outdoor lights, the water rippling gently in the evening breeze. Beyond the pool, the city of Los Angeles sprawled out before him, the Hollywood sign perched on the hills in the distance like some great monument to nothing. He had spent his life trying to conquer this city, trying to build an empire that would outlast him. But now, as he stood there, staring out at the skyline, it all felt hollow. Meaningless.

He sat down heavily on one of the pool chairs, the cushion sinking under his weight. The lapping of the water against the edge of the pool was soothing, almost hypnotic. It reminded him of the ocean, the one place where he had ever felt at peace. He closed his eyes and let the sound wash over him, pushing away the memories, and the regrets.

His mind drifted back to his sons, to the mess they had made of everything. Jace, with his weakness, his constant need for approval. And Cole, so full of rage, so desperate to prove something—to him, to the world, to himself. He had wanted so much for them, wanted them to succeed where he had failed. But they had become nothing more than reflections of his failures. He wasn't angry at them, not really. He was angry at himself. Angry at the father who had beaten him into submission, angry at the family that had pushed him down this path. It was all a cycle, wasn't it? A vicious, endless cycle of fathers and sons, of broken promises and shattered dreams.

As he sat there, staring out at the city, a strange sense of calm settled over him. The anger that had fueled him for so long was fading, replaced by something quieter, something more profound. He realized, in that moment, that none of it mattered. The power, the wealth, the endless struggle to prove himself—it was all for nothing. No one would remember him. No one would remember any of this. His sons would fall, just like he had. His empire would crumble. And one day, the world would move on, forgetting them entirely.

It was a sobering thought, but not a painful one. He had spent his entire life trying to outrun the inevitable, trying to make something permanent in a world that was anything but. But now, with his life in ruins, and his family destroyed, he felt a strange sort of freedom. None of it mattered. It never had.

He smiled then, a small, sad smile, as he leaned back in the chair and let the breeze wash over him. The palm trees swayed gently in the wind, their leaves rustling like whispers from another world. He had always loved the sound of the wind through the trees, the way it made everything feel alive, even when nothing was.

For the first time in years, he felt at peace. The world would forget him, forget his sons, forget everything they had done. And that was okay. There was a certain beauty in that, in the fleeting nature of life, in the way everything eventually returned to dust.

He closed his eyes, letting the cool night air lull him into a sense of calm. The lapping of the pool water became the only sound he heard, a gentle rhythm that echoed in his mind. All the pain, all the regret, it didn't matter anymore.

And as the lights of Hollywood flickered in the distance, he let himself smile.

18

HOME

C OLE

1987 - One Year Later

Cole sat in the courtroom, his wrists shackled, his eyes fixed on the cold, sterile floor beneath him. The words of the judge echoed in his ears like distant thunder—guilty on all counts. Three counts of first-degree murder, one of them an LAPD officer. There was no point in fighting it; the evidence was overwhelming, the trial swift. His life, which had spiraled out of control for years, had finally crashed to a halt. The sentence was life without parole. He would die in prison.

As he was led from the courthouse, his mind drifted. He had never felt so empty, so drained. The rage, the anger, even the twisted sense of purpose that had fueled him for so long had disappeared, leaving only a vast hollow inside him. The thought of Jace and Clay briefly crossed his mind, but it didn't sting the way it used to. There was only numbness now. And perhaps, a small flicker of relief.

The prison was a different world, one Cole had dreaded but also accepted long before the trial began. On his first day, the guards stripped him down, searched him, and threw him into a small cell with a man named Dante, a hulking figure. The prison was a harsh place, filled with predators and broken men. Cole knew he had to keep his head down and avoid drawing attention. But there was no hiding who he was anymore.

Weeks passed. The routine was mind-numbing. Wake up, eat, exercise, stare at the walls, repeat. Every day, the weight of his past crimes seemed to press harder on his chest, suffocating him. He felt the crushing burden of expectations, the legacy of his father, and the guilt of Jace's suffering. But there, in that tiny, grimy cell, no one cared about any of that. There were no judgments, no harsh words. Only the slow march toward oblivion.

One night, after the lights went out, Dante leaned over from the bunk above and whispered, "You ever let yourself be real, Cole?" Cole froze. There was a charge in the air, something that made the hairs on his neck stand on end. He didn't answer. He didn't know how to.

Without waiting for a response, Dante climbed down from his bunk, his massive figure casting a shadow over Cole. "Ain't nobody watchin' here. No one cares who you used to be out there. In here, you belong to yourself... or to me." The words were heavy, weighted with something Cole had never allowed himself to feel.

In the dim light of the cell, Dante pushed Cole onto his stomach. For the first time in his life, Cole didn't resist.

There was no fight left in him. He wasn't thinking about his father, or Jace, or the weight of the world pressing down on him. He let it happen, surrendering to something primal, something raw. As Dante took him, there was no judgment, no shame. Just a strange sense of peace.

It was rough and brutal, but it didn't feel wrong. For the first time, Cole felt like he didn't have to pretend, didn't have to wear the mask he'd been forced to wear his entire life. Here, in this broken world, he could just exist, stripped of everything that had once defined him. His father's expectations, the criminal empire, the lies—it all fell away.

When it was over, Dante returned to his bunk without a word, and Cole lay there, breathing heavily in the dark. His body ached, but his mind was strangely calm. He had been used. But in some twisted way, it was a relief. There was no hate, no judgment in Dante's touch. Only need. And for once, Cole felt like he wasn't alone in that need.

This was his new reality. A place where he could stop pretending. Where he could just be.

19

THE LETTER

JACE'S LETTER

Clay,

By the time you read this, it might already be too late. I don't know how this will end, but there's a feeling in my gut that I can't ignore anymore. I think I've always known this would happen—ever since we first met since I first laid eyes on you, and everything changed. You were the one real thing in a life that's been nothing but lies and shadows. I didn't deserve you, but I loved you the best way I could.

I've been a coward, Clay. I know that. I've let Cole, our father, and the entire family name chain me to this life, and I've done things I'm not proud of. You wanted me to be free, to get out, but I couldn't. I've spent my whole life looking up to Cole, trying to survive in the shadow of someone I can never be. And in doing that, I lost who I am.

I never told you how much I envy you. You're strong in ways I could never be. You were willing to walk away from everything—your family, your past, even me—just to try to live a life on your terms. And I've been stuck here, trying to please everyone, even when I knew it was killing me. I see that now. You were right. I couldn't see it before, but you were always right.

There are things I've kept from you—things I didn't know how to tell you. About Cole. About our father. About the way this family works. I've been protecting them, covering up for them, even though I knew it was wrong. Cole... he's not just my brother. He's my tormentor. He's made sure I've suffered for every inch of freedom I've tried to take, and he'll never stop. I thought I could handle it. I thought I could keep it all separate—keep you safe from it— but I see now that was a lie. A dangerous lie.

I DON'T KNOW what Cole's planning, but I'm scared, Clay. Not just for me—for you, too. He knows. He knows everything about us, about your plans, about the way you've tried to get me to leave him behind. He's been watching us, keeping tabs, and I can't let him hurt you. Not like he's hurt me.

I've written this letter because I need you to know the truth. I've loved you, Clay, more than I've ever loved anyone. But that love has been poisoned by this family, by the life I was born into. I've lied to you by staying. I should've left with you when I had the chance. I should've taken your hand and run away from this place, from this mess. I was too weak to do it, and for that, I'm sorry.

I'm sorry for the things I'll never be able to fix. I'm sorry for the pain I've caused you. I'm sorry I couldn't be the man you needed me to be.

But above all else, I want you to know that what we had—what we shared—was real. Don't ever doubt that. Don't ever doubt how much I wanted it to last, how much I wanted to be the man who could stand beside you without looking over his shoulder. I wanted that life, Clay. I wanted it more than anything.

I don't know what's coming next. Maybe it's the end for me. Maybe it's the end for both of us. But if I don't make it out of this, if something happens, I need you to survive. I need you to live the life I couldn't. Don't let Cole or anyone else take that away from you. You're stronger than this. Stronger than me. Don't let them bury you the way they buried me.

If this is goodbye, I want you to remember me as the man who loved you, not the one who failed you. I hope you can forgive me one day.

Yours, always,

Jace

20

FREEDOM

Miriam

1990 - Three Years Later

She sat on the porch of a small cottage nestled deep in the woods of northern California. She had chosen this place carefully, away from the sprawling madness of Los Angeles, away from her husband, her son, and all the noise. She sipped her tea, watching as the fog rolled over the hills in the early morning light. It was peaceful here, tranquil in a way she had never known before. For the first time in decades, she could hear herself think.

It wasn't that she didn't love Clay. She had. At least, she had tried to. But there was something hollow in her love, something she could never quite fill, no matter how hard she worked to be the wife and mother they all expected her to be. And her husband—well, that had been a prison of its own making. She had been a good wife, a loyal wife, but she had been dying in that house for years.

People always think it's the dramatic moments that break you, Miriam thought, but it wasn't. It was the quiet ones. The moments in between the yelling, the fights, the apologies. It was the silence that had finally done her in. One day, she had just stood up from the kitchen table and walked out. No note, no explanation. Just left. Her husband hadn't followed her, and that was the final confirmation she needed that she had been right to go.

Maybe something had snapped in her, or maybe she had finally woken up after all those years of sleepwalking through life. Either way, she didn't regret it. Not for one moment. She had rebuilt herself here, in the quiet wilderness, free from the weight of expectations. Her husband, and her son, were distant memories now, fragments of a life that felt foreign to her.

Miriam had learned something important since she left: control was an illusion, but the ability to change—really change—wasn't. She couldn't change the world. She couldn't change the people in her life, no matter how much she had wanted to fix Clay or make her husband softer, kinder. But she could change herself. And that had been enough.

She didn't feel guilty about abandoning Clay. Darkly funny, that. Shouldn't she have? A mother was supposed to be consumed by guilt, by longing to fix what had gone wrong. But she didn't. It wasn't that she didn't care about him—she did, in some strange, detached way. But that life, that version of her, felt so far away. And the truth was, some people just didn't have it in them to fix what was broken. She had tried. But not anymore.

The birds were singing now, the sun finally breaking through the mist. Miriam sat back in her chair, letting the warmth of the day settle over her like a blanket. She had been free for nearly three years now. It felt longer. Time moved differently here. The seasons changed in ways she had never paid attention to when she lived in Los Angeles. It was strange how life had a way of slipping past you when you weren't paying attention.

She wondered, sometimes, what had become of Clay. If he had stayed in that world she had escaped, or if he had found his way out. She doubted it. He was too much like his father—trapped in the chaos, in the violence. But it didn't matter. It couldn't matter anymore.

Miriam had learned to let go. To sever the ties that had once bound her so tightly. She had to, or she would have been dragged down with them. She wasn't the kind of woman who could live like that anymore. Maybe she never had been.

As the day wore on, she stood and walked inside the cottage, leaving the quiet behind her. There was a storm coming tonight. She could feel it in the air. But here, in her sanctuary, storms were a comfort, a reminder that nature, too, had its way of resetting itself, of washing away what needed to be forgotten. She was part of that cycle now.

FREE.

AFTERWORD

In a world where we are taught that family is the cornerstone of everything, the foundation on which we are meant to build our lives, it's easy to believe that having a family—maintaining one, protecting it—is the ultimate goal. The stories we are raised with, and the expectations we inherit, tell us that without family, we are incomplete. But what happens when family becomes the very thing that chains us, that pulls us into cycles of pain, toxicity, and trauma?

Fading Into Silence is, at its heart, a story about the unraveling of these illusions. It's about two men, Jace and Clay, whose lives are so deeply entangled with the expectations of family, that they cannot see a way out—until they do. And it's about Cole, who, like many, is a tragic product of the very thing he despises yet clings to, a symbol of the generational trauma that so often defines the concept of family.

We spend so much of our lives trying to define what family is supposed to mean. For some, it is love, safety, and a source of strength. For others, it's a burden, a legacy of wounds and scars passed down from one generation to the next. We often hear the phrase "family is everything," but is it? Should it be? The pressure to hold on to something harmful—simply because it is labeled "family"—can be more damaging than walking away.

The reality is that family, in its most traditional sense, isn't for everyone. The idea that family is the ultimate goal, that it'sthe be-all and end-all of life, is a concept that doesn't fit the narrative of everyone's journey. For some, it is a chosen family that brings them peace. For others, freedom lies in breaking away, severing ties, in rejecting the expectations that have been placed upon them from birth.

We often don't talk enough about the mental health repercussions of staying in toxic family dynamics. How much of what we consider "family loyalty" is just generational trauma passed down, waiting to be recycled in the next group of lives? To dismantle the very idea of family that has been used to control, to hurt, to mold us into something we are not.

This isn't a condemnation of family itself. For many, family is a place of healing, of belonging, of deep and unconditional love. But it is also an acknowledgment that not all families are built the same. Some families, like the one in this story, are toxic ecosystems where emotional, psychological, and even physical survival is a constant battle. And for those in such situations, the greatest act of self-love can be the decision to walk away.

STAY TUNED

OUT OF THE CLOSET

Don't be a follower.

Coming Soon

ABOUT THE AUTHOR

Nicholas Michael Matiz is a bold voice in the realm of Gay fiction, known for his gritty, raw storytelling that pushes boundaries and explores the darker sides of human nature.

Milton Keynes UK
Ingram Content Group UK Ltd.
UKHW021937281024
450365UK00018B/1129